Jamie sat

"Yes, Dani... you... have to accept that.
There are some things in this world that your
money can't buy, and I'm one of them."

"Did I say anything about money?"

"It's implied. You're so used to getting your
way that you forget other people have free
will."

"Let me rephrase, then. I don't accept that
you don't want to find the man who took
two lives and ruined two others... That
doesn't excite you?"

She took her time answering. "I would be
pleased to prosecute that man as part of my
job. But for me, it's not personal."

"So this case is nothing personal? Just
business?"

She nodded curtly.

"What was that kiss all about, then?"

Her gaze locked with his. Jamie licked
her lips and swallowed. "Th-that kiss is
immaterial to this discussion. We were
talking about the justice system. Our work."

"You're right. Immaterial. Completely out of
line for me to even bring it up." With that,
he leaned in and kissed her again.

Dear Reader,

Revenge is an ugly thing. I guess that's why it works so well as a motivation in a novel—it creates instant internal conflict. If the author does her job, the reader will share the character's outrage and totally understand the desire to strike back; at the same time, the reader knows that taking the law into your own hands is wrong.

Creating that inner conflict is why I write novels. I find it delicious!

In this story, my hero, Daniel, feels a strong desire to strike back at the person who framed him for murder, causing him to spend six miserable years on death row. What better heroine to give him than a law-and-order prosecutor? I hope you enjoy the long journey each of them has to make before they can be together for the long haul.

Best,

Kara Lennox

A Score to Settle
Kara Lennox

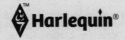

TORONTO NEW YORK LONDON
AMSTERDAM PARIS SYDNEY HAMBURG
STOCKHOLM ATHENS TOKYO MILAN MADRID
PRAGUE WARSAW BUDAPEST AUCKLAND

Recycling programs
for this product may
not exist in your area.

ISBN-13: 978-0-373-71701-9

A SCORE TO SETTLE

Printed in U.S.A.

ABOUT THE AUTHOR

Kara Lennox has earned her living at various times as an art director, typesetter, textbook editor and reporter. She's worked in a boutique, a health club and an ad agency. She's been an antiques dealer, an artist and even a blackjack dealer. But no work has ever made her happier than writing romance novels. To date, she has written more than sixty books. Kara is a recent transplant to Southern California. When not writing, she indulges in an ever-changing array of hobbies. Her latest passions are bird-watching, long-distance bicycling, vintage jewelry and, by necessity, do-it-yourself home renovation. She loves to hear from readers; you can find her at www.karalennox.com.

Books by Kara Lennox

HARLEQUIN SUPERROMANCE

1689—TAKEN TO THE EDGE#
1695—NOTHING BUT THE TRUTH#

HARLEQUIN AMERICAN ROMANCE

974—FORTUNE'S TWINS
990—THE MILLIONAIRE NEXT DOOR
1052—THE FORGOTTEN COWBOY
1068—HOMETOWN HONEY*
1081—DOWNTOWN DEBUTANTE*
1093—OUT OF TOWN BRIDE*
1146—THE FAMILY RESCUE**
1150—HER PERFECT HERO**
1154—AN HONORABLE MAN**
1180—ONE STUBBORN TEXAN
1195—GOOD HUSBAND MATERIAL
1216—RELUCTANT PARTNERS††
1240—THE PREGNANCY SURPRISE††
1256—THE GOOD FATHER††

#Project Justice
*Blond Justice
**Firehouse 59
††Second Sons

For my sister Pat.

You are so good at everything.
I wouldn't be the person I am today if I hadn't
tried so hard to keep up with you.

CHAPTER ONE

JAMIE McNAIR FUMED SILENTLY as she crawled along a traffic-clogged Houston freeway. Who did Daniel Logan think he was, summoning her as if she was one of his lackeys? When she'd heard that the billionaire wanted to overturn one of *her* verdicts, she'd been anxious to talk to him and set him straight. But on her terms, not his.

Unfortunately, he'd gone over her head, which tweaked her all the more. Now, because her boss was scared of Daniel and his charitable foundation, she had to make a command performance.

A meeting at the Project Justice office would have been tolerable. But no, Logan had decided he wanted to meet her at his home.

She hated being manipulated. But since Logan had forced her into this meeting, she intended to make it count. In her briefcase she had every piece of information she needed to convince Logan that Christopher Gables was right where he belonged—on death row for brutally killing his business partner.

She had far better things to do than cater to the whims of a spoiled, supposedly do-gooder billionaire. Logan might be wealthy and powerful, but he was also a convicted murderer himself. Her own father had prosecuted Daniel many years ago, and her dad hadn't been one to make mistakes.

To prepare for the meeting, she had learned everything she could about Logan. She'd found lots of data about his arrest and trial, as well as his family's oil company. Unfortunately, personal information was in short supply.

The most recent picture she had found was a blurry wire-service photo of him the day he was released from prison six years ago. Back then, he'd been a tall, thin, pale man with a bad haircut. In photos from his trial—more than twelve years ago—he'd looked like a handsome but scared frat boy.

A few minutes later she pulled up to a set of ornate wrought-iron gates in tony River Oaks, one of the richest zip codes in America. She was steamed, but she couldn't deny a certain curiosity to see the inside of this place. From the outside, it looked like a nineteenth-century English estate home, something that might be found in a Jane Austen novel, complete with ivy-covered walls and worn cobbles forming the driveway.

Jamie was about to get out of her car and walk up to the intercom when the gates opened quietly on well-oiled hinges. She pulled her car—an aging Subaru that must have looked as out of place as a donkey in church—down the cobbled driveway toward the house.

When she got out, one of her heels caught in the cobbles and she turned her ankle. *Good night.* Who made their driveway out of real cobblestones? Limping slightly and silently cursing at the added annoyance, she made her way to the front door; two huge panels of carved oak that looked as if they belonged on an ancient castle.

She reached for the bell, but before she could press it the door opened.

"Ms. McNair, please come in."

Standing in the doorway was a beautiful young woman with a sleek, blond bob. She wore a snug lavender cashmere sweater, skinny black pants and pointy-toed boots. Though Jamie wasn't exactly a clotheshorse, she knew quality when she saw it.

Even Daniel's servants were well-to-do.

"Thank you. You must be Jillian." Jamie had recognized the slight British accent as belonging to Daniel Logan's personal assistant.

Inside, the foyer was no less impressive than the outside, soaring three stories to a peaked roof with stained-glass windows that shot beams of colorful light to the white marble floor below. At the center of the foyer was a fountain in the shape of a boy riding a sea horse, like something one might find in ancient Greece. On the walls were oil paintings in gilt frames, museum-quality portraits and landscapes.

Holy mother of…was that a Van Gogh?

"You're a few minutes late," Jillian said matter-of-factly.

"Yes. The traffic…" Jamie was damned if she was

going to apologize for being twenty minutes late when Logan was the one who had insisted she meet him here, rather than at his downtown office, which was within walking distance of her own workplace at the Criminal Justice Center.

"Unfortunately, Mr. Logan had another appointment. He should be free in about an hour. In the meanwhile, I'm sure you'd like some lunch."

Jamie was starved, but she wasn't going to let Logan's underling lead her around by the nose. "Unfortunately," Jamie said, enunciating every word, "my time is limited as well, and the traffic jam tightened my schedule. If Mr. Logan can't see me right now, perhaps he can come by my office when it's convenient for him."

Jillian's eyes widened slightly. Probably she was so used to people bowing and scraping, eager to please her high-and-mighty boss, that Jamie's behavior came as a surprise.

"Give me a minute and I'll see what can be arranged." Her tone had gone a bit frosty.

Jillian stepped out of the foyer, leaving Jamie alone and steaming. Just because she was a public servant didn't mean Logan could treat her as if she were insignificant. She would walk right out of here and see how he liked it.

Jamie turned toward a noise she heard in the doorway, thinking Jillian had returned, but instead it was a large golden retriever. Tongue lolling, tail wagging, he accelerated toward her, and for a moment she thought he was going to jump up on her. But he skidded to a stop mere inches from her and stared up at her with big chocolate-brown eyes.

"Oh. Hello, there." She reached out cautiously to pat his head. He looked friendly, but you could never tell with dogs. This one wagged half his body, obviously thrilled by her scant attention. He leaned into her, and she scratched him behind the ear.

Jillian finally reappeared. "Tucker. Behave."

The dog obediently abandoned Jamie and trotted to Jillian, sitting at her heel, and she gave him an absent pat on the head. He was obviously well trained.

"Mr. Logan will see you now. But he apologizes for his rather, um, casual attire."

He could be dressed in a potato sack for all Jamie cared. She just wanted to get this meeting over with. Having tangled with Project Justice before, she knew that the foundation often took on cases that had merit.

This wasn't one of them.

With the dog following them, Jillian led Jamie through an opulent living room, a strange study in contrasts—ancient-looking tapestries and modernist furniture; cold marble and a warm sandstone fireplace; an antique, ivory-inlaid table here and a modern one of polished limestone there.

She got only a quick impression. Soon they were walking down a long hallway lined with more paintings, and finally down a flight of stairs.

He had a basement?

This just didn't seem normal. What had she gotten herself into? Logan might be a refined gentleman, but he was also a convicted murderer. The governor had pardoned him, but the conviction had never been overturned—a distinction that made Jamie feel edgy about meeting him in an underground bunker.

Finally, they ended up in an enormous workout room with fancy machines worthy of any upscale health club. But what drew her eye was the naked man lying on a massage table, getting worked over by a busty blonde in a pink velour tracksuit.

Jamie sucked in a long breath. He had only a small towel over his hips to preserve his modesty.

"Daniel, Ms. McNair is here." Jillian sounded faintly disapproving.

"Ow, Greta, have a heart," said the naked man, who Jamie assumed was Daniel Logan.

He was still tall, but no longer skinny or pale. In fact, the large expanse of skin on his muscular back was an even golden color, and for a moment she wished with all her heart that she was Greta, digging her fingers into those firm-looking muscles.

Daniel turned his head and caught sight of Jamie for the first time. Their eyes locked and held for several seconds.

He was arrestingly gorgeous, and he looked nothing like the stereotypical Texas billionaire in the oil bidness. No boots, no hat, no cigar and no Texas twang. His voice was cultured, educated.

"I'm afraid you've caught me at my worst, Ms. McNair," he said. "But I got a muscle spasm in my back just before you arrived, and Greta is the only person who can get rid of it."

Yeah, and he probably got *lots* of muscle spasms.

"Mr. Logan," Jamie said succinctly. "We can't have an intelligent discussion under these conditions. I suggest that if this meeting is important to you, we reschedule. Or even speak on the phone. You can call my office—"

"No, wait, please." Daniel pushed himself up on his strong-looking arms and swung his legs over the massage table, somehow managing to wrap the towel around himself in the process so that he didn't flash the three women surrounding him. "I can meet with you now."

Greta handed him a silk robe, which he donned as he hopped off the table, letting the towel drop to the carpet. He shrugged experimentally, stretched his neck side to side and smiled. "I think you did it, Greta. Now, if you don't mind giving us a bit of privacy?" He included Jillian in his request.

Greta melted away as quietly as an icicle in the hot sun, but Jillian hesitated. "Are you sure you don't need me to take notes? Or bring you a file?"

"That won't be necessary for this meeting, thanks." He leaned down to scratch the dog, which had been waiting patiently for some attention from him. "Hey, Tucker."

With one last warning scowl toward Jamie, Jillian walked away.

"My office is this way," Daniel said. "Thank you for coming. It won't be a waste of your time—I think you'll be interested in what I have to say."

Jamie was dumbfounded by the luxury she saw all around her. In a basement, no less. Though they were underground, what appeared to be natural light surrounded them, pouring in from windows and skylights covered with frosted glass or translucent shades. But the most impressive sight was Daniel Logan himself.

He literally made her mouth go dry. No sign of a bad haircut now. As soon as he'd moved to an upright position, his silky brown hair had fallen into place perfectly. The hair was a medium length on top and short over his ears, where he had a sprinkling of premature gray.

Her research had told her he was in his mid-thirties, but he looked slightly older. Not that that was a bad thing. He was still handsome as sin. Perhaps prison had aged him.

She stopped herself before she started feeling sorry for him. He was a convicted murderer who belonged behind bars. Because of his money and influence, he was free to enjoy all this luxury.

His victim, Andreas Musto, would never enjoy anything again.

Daniel's office was another surprise. She'd expected a commanding antique walnut desk or maybe a workspace carved from a solid piece of granite, and walls decorated with more original art, perhaps a giant, saltwater fish tank or a bearskin rug—something masculine. Instead, she found herself in a high-tech cave.

She'd never seen so much electronic equipment in one place outside a Best Buy. A huge U-shaped desk dominated the room, littered with gadgets of every description: multiple phones, keyboards, printers, three computers, each of which appeared to be in use. One of them had a monitor the size of a movie-theater screen.

Mounted on the walls above them were four TVs, each tuned to a different news channel.

Daniel indicated that Jamie should sit in one of the silk-covered wingback chairs facing the desk. He moved around the room to take his place in the giant rolling chair inside the U. Tucker settled onto a big pillow where he could watch his master with adoring eyes.

For all its high-tech feel, the room was still beautiful. More faux windows covered with black, wooden shutters lined one wall. A fine Oriental carpet topped the wood floor, and above them, two stained-glass chandeliers bathed them in warm light.

"Perhaps we can just cut to the chase here," Jamie said, wanting to get in the first word. "You have some wild idea that Christopher Gables is innocent. I don't know what might have led you down that garden path, but I can assure you, the facts speak for themselves. Gables and his victim argued. A couple of hours later, the victim was found dead with a slashed throat, a bloody knife lying nearby. Gables's prints—and only his prints—were found on the knife.

"Gables, who was normally in the restaurant until closing, could not account for his whereabouts at the time of the murder.

"That, Mr. Logan, is what we in the prosecution business call a slam dunk. The jury reached a verdict in less than an hour."

Daniel Logan seemed to be listening intently. He kept his gaze firmly focused on her as she spoke, his expression grave, nodding every so often. It unnerved her, having that laser beam of attention pointed at her, and she got the impression he was not only listening to her words, but observing every nuance of her face, her gestures—and learning more than she wanted him to know.

"So what do you have to wow me with, Mr. Logan?" she asked, struggling to keep from sounding smug. "If it's that little bit of unidentified DNA found on Sissom's apron, you should know that fingerprints trump DNA any day. Four separate fingerprint experts identified the prints on the knife as belonging to Gables—even the defense's own expert witness. The DNA could have come from anywhere."

Logan nodded again. "It was a solid case. You did an excellent job prosecuting."

Yes, she had. It had been the first big case in which she'd led the prosecution. After the verdict, for the first time in her life, she'd felt sure her father was proud of her. Not that she would ever know for sure, since he had died while she was in law school.

She did not thank Logan for the compliment. Flattery wouldn't sway her. "So, what's your point?"

"Ms. McNair, how would you like to prosecute a serial killer?"

DANIEL COULD SEE HE'D GOTTEN Jamie's attention. His initial salvo was a shock tactic, sure; he'd have to have the facts to back up his claim. But at least she'd dropped that infuriating smugness. Her pouty lips were open slightly in surprise, her eyes wide and attentive.

He hadn't expected her to be so beautiful in person. But the photos and video he'd seen didn't do her justice. The glossy, fudge-brown hair had depth and texture no camera could pick up; the unusual shade of blue-green in her eyes defied description. And her skin—like the smoothest stone—somehow also looked warm to the touch.

He told himself it was best for him not to think about her lips too much.

All that was above the neck. He didn't dare study her anywhere else until her attention was diverted.

Finally she spoke. "You think Christopher Gables has killed before?" She barely whispered the possibility.

"No. I think whoever killed Frank Sissom—and framed Christopher—has killed before. He's the same man who framed me."

At last Jamie found her voice. "You have got to be

kidding. You brought me all the way here, disrupted my whole day's schedule, so you could hit me with this... this *ridiculous* fairy tale about a serial killer?"

"It's still an unproven theory, I'll admit. But aren't you the least bit curious as to why I'm trying to convince you it's true?"

"Because you like manipulating people, and you have the money and influence to do it?"

He bit the inside of his lower lip to hold on to his temper. Typical prosecutor. She was so sure she was right, that the almighty justice system was infallible. "You seem a bit cranky this morning. You probably haven't had enough protein. Let me guess—you skipped breakfast."

"My diet is no concern of yours. Are we done here?" She started to rise from her chair.

"Metal shavings. Were any metal shavings found on Frank Sissom's body?" It was one of two anomalies brought to light during Daniel's own murder trial. The prosecution never successfully explained where those shavings had come from, but Daniel had always believed they'd come from the murderer's own clothing during a struggle.

These days, metal shavings could be analyzed every which way right down to their atoms. Every metal object had a distinct signature, so shavings could be matched to their source. It wasn't perfect, not like DNA or fingerprints. But cases had been won and lost based on similar trace evidence.

The other anomaly was, in fact, a bit of unidentified DNA found on Andreas's clothing. Another similarity to the Gables/Sissom case, which Jamie herself had just mentioned.

"I don't recall hearing about any metal shavings," Jamie said.

Daniel tried not to be too disappointed. It was a long shot. "Let me go over the facts, then, as I see them."

Jamie glanced at her watch. "I have other appointments today. You can put your so-called facts in an email."

Just then someone tapped on Daniel's office door. He knew that tap. Everyone knocked on doors differently. It was one of those patterns that Daniel had picked up without trying.

"Come in, Jillian."

She entered, holding a plate with a metal warming lid over it in one hand, and a tall glass of iced tea in the other. "I am so sorry to interrupt, but Claude insists this chicken will go bad if it's not eaten immediately. Something about the sauce coagulating."

It was past Daniel's usual lunchtime; the muscle spasm—and Jamie's tardiness—had put a kink in his schedule. Jillian knew he put great stock in eating well and often to fuel the brain. But she also knew not to interrupt an important meeting.

He accepted the plate from her. "Thank you, Jillian, but it would be excessively rude for me to eat in front of my guest. Especially since she hasn't had breakfast."

"I never said I skipped breakfast," Jamie objected.

"But you did." He knew he was right just by the slight shade of defensiveness in her tone.

"Of course I brought a plate for Ms. McNair." Jillian quickly produced another covered dish from a rolling cart she'd left in the hallway.

"I'm not staying," Jamie said.

"Give me fifteen minutes to convince you." Daniel stood and came out from behind his desk. "Share a meal with me. You've got to eat at some point, and this will save you time." *And probably improve your temperament.* Also, sharing food was a bonding activity. He needed to convince Jamie that he was not the enemy. If things went his way, they would soon become allies, fighting to save an innocent man's life. As the prosecutor of this case, she was uniquely able to handle some tasks he would find difficult to do himself.

Jamie inhaled deeply; she probably had gotten a whiff of whatever genius concoction Claude, his chef, had whipped up today, because something convinced her.

"Fine, if you insist, I'll have some lunch. But keep in mind you can't soften me up with a gourmet meal."

No, but good food could make her more open to his suggestions.

Jillian set up their lunch in the small room adjacent to Daniel's office, where he sometimes took his meals when he was deep into a project and didn't want to go all the way upstairs to the dining room or patio. He'd had it specially designed to relieve stress.

Although it had no windows, he'd had lights installed that replicated the electromagnetic spectrum of sunlight. The limestone floor and running-water feature helped to ionize the air, and all the plants, of course, provided an oxygen-rich environment.

"Good night!" Jamie paused at the doorway, her jaw about to hit the floor.

CHAPTER TWO

"SOMETHING WRONG?" Daniel asked innocently as Jillian placed napkins and silverware on the wrought-iron umbrella table.

Jamie shook her head in obvious amazement. "Oh, nothing, just that I thought for a moment I'd walked through a wormhole and was transported to an outdoor café in Tuscany. This is incredible!"

"I'm glad you like it." Daniel enjoyed surprising people.

"Are those…grapes?" Jamie looked above them at the grape arbor, which did, indeed, have a few clusters of fruit growing on it.

"Yes, they are. I had some of our grapevines transplanted to this room. I wasn't sure they'd survive—grapes are tricky. But they seem to love it here."

"Where did you get that fountain?" she asked suspiciously.

"From an antiquities dealer. Legal, I assure you. It was recovered in pieces from an Italian farmer's field. The restoration cost more than the fountain did. Shall we eat?"

Daniel pulled out a chair for Jamie, then took his

own. He did love this room. Already, he could feel some of the tension leaving his body. He shrugged, testing his back, but the muscle spasm appeared to be gone for good.

Sometimes he took for granted what his wealth could create.

Jillian took Tucker and departed, leaving Daniel and Jamie alone.

Daniel lifted the lid on his plate and inhaled. His mouth watered. "I'll have to find out the name of this dish so I can request it again."

"It does smell good," Jamie said cautiously as she examined her own plate. It was a small portion of chicken with a light dousing of creamy sauce, along with a generous helping of fresh asparagus and some rosemary new potatoes.

Daniel cut a piece off the chicken, but his attention was focused more closely on Jamie than his meat. He wanted her to enjoy the food.

She took a bite, chewed thoughtfully, swallowed. "Your fifteen minutes are running."

"Right." Damn, he'd almost forgotten the reason she was here. Who cared if she liked Claude's cooking? It was more important that she like his facts.

"Are you familiar with the Andreas Musto murder case?"

"The one for which you stood trial. I'm somewhat well versed," she said cautiously. Which probably meant that what she knew, she'd absorbed from the media. It had been one of those crimes that reporters loved to sensationalize—a billionaire's son accused of a gruesome slaying.

"I'll quickly refresh your memory. Andreas Musto was my business partner. We owned a restaurant together. He was found at the restaurant with his throat cut, the murder weapon—a wickedly sharp butcher knife—lying nearby. The knife had my fingerprints on it. I did not have an alibi. Does this sound at all familiar?"

Jamie, who had been devouring her rosemary potatoes during his speech, made a show of chewing, swallowing, taking a sip of iced tea and delicately blotting her mouth with her napkin.

"I'll admit, the circumstances are similar to those of the Frank Sissom murder. But lots of crimes sound alike. There are only so many ways to kill people—shooting, stabbing, poisoning, strangling, drowning or blunt-force trauma."

"But how many killers—seemingly intelligent young men like myself and Christopher Gables—leave behind the murder weapon with their prints on it?"

"Criminals often act without logic. In the heat of the moment, a person can lose their ability to reason. Take the bank robber who wrote the demand note on his own deposit slip. Or the man who, hours after a murder, goes on a spending spree with the victim's credit cards."

"And just how many murder victims have their throats slashed with a butcher knife? In a restaurant?"

"Murders often take place in restaurants. They're open late at night, they deal in cash—"

"Robbery wasn't the motive in either case."

"The crimes took place many years apart," Jamie said sensibly. "The locations were twenty, maybe thirty miles from each other. I'm sorry, but the facts do not scream 'serial killer' to me."

He was losing her. He could see it in her eyes.

"So this is why Project Justice took on Christopher Gables as a client?" she asked. "The crime reminded you of the one that landed you in prison?"

"Partly." He'd rather not tell Jamie about Theresa Chavez until he interviewed the woman himself. But he had to do something to make an impression.

"The similarities in the crimes are one reason I took the case," he admitted. His decision had shocked his staff; he'd never personally led an investigation before. "It was easy for me to put myself in Christopher's place. But what really swayed me was the witness."

"Witness? There was no witness."

"Ah, but there was. A young woman who bussed tables at the restaurant, El Toreador. She called the police, babbling incoherently in Spanish, then fled the scene before she could be interviewed."

Jamie leaned back in her chair. "Theresa Chavez. She was the one we think found the body," Jamie said. "That's not the same as a witness to the murder."

"So you know about her." Damn, he'd been hoping to take Jamie by surprise.

"She was considered briefly as a suspect, but dismissed because she was hardly more than a teenager and weighed a hundred pounds soaking wet. Frank Sissom was six foot and two-twenty. No way she could have overpowered him."

"But she was never questioned."

"Unfortunately, Theresa was an illegal alien. Apparently she was scared of being deported, so she went into hiding. We never found her."

"How hard did you look?"

"The police made a concerted effort to locate her." Jamie didn't conceal her defensiveness very well. "But a person with no credit cards, no social security number or driver's license—she disappeared. Completely."

"But not forever. Theresa has recently come forward. Her conscience was bothering her. She says she spotted a stranger in the restaurant kitchen only minutes before Frank was killed. It certainly wasn't Christopher Gables, whom she knew quite well."

His news did not have the desired effect. Jamie did not look shocked or even surprised. She raised one skeptical eyebrow. "After what, six years? Her conscience is bothering her?"

He supposed he couldn't blame Jamie for her skepticism. Her job put her in daily contact with criminals of the worst order, most of whom would do or say anything to get them off the hook.

"It's more like a change of circumstances," Daniel said, noting with some satisfaction that Jamie was well on the way to cleaning her plate. "Her conscience has always bothered her. But she recently got a green card. She doesn't have to fear deportation. Her English has also improved a great deal in the last seven years."

"Well. If she has something to say, I'd like to hear it." Jamie's tone indicated she didn't want to hear it at all, but didn't want to be considered unreasonable. "Have her contact my office. I will at least listen to what she has to say."

"Will you really?"

"If I say I will, then I will. But keep in mind, eyewitness testimony isn't the gold standard it once was. So many things can taint a person's memories—the passage of time, the influence of the media or others' recollections, even a fervent wish to have seen something different. And, of course, the promise of a load of cash can improve a person's memory in sudden and dramatic ways."

This was the height of rudeness. "You think I would pay someone to— You're actually accusing me of—"

"I am not accusing anyone," she said hastily. "Just stating a few well-known facts about witness testimony in general. I'm willing to hear the woman's statement. But I will accept hard, physical evidence over witness testimony any day."

"Are you saying an eyewitness to the crime wouldn't convince you to reopen a case?"

"I won't know until I actually talk to this Theresa.

I mean, how will I know she's even the same person, since she had no documentation back then?"

"We'll cross that bridge, trust me."

"That's just the problem. I don't trust you. I don't trust anyone with an ax to grind."

At least he and Jamie had that in common. Daniel didn't trust anyone, either, at least not beyond his senior staff at Project Justice and in his own home. He wouldn't begrudge Jamie that mistrust. "All I ask is that you give the woman a chance to speak."

"If she'll call my office and make an appointment, I'll meet with her." Jamie popped the last bit of asparagus into her mouth, chewing with a satisfied expression.

This was the best Daniel could expect. Having reached the terms he'd hoped for, it was time to end this meeting. He had learned long ago that once someone agreed with him, the best course of action was to get the hell away from them before he said or did something to change their mind.

But he was loath to send Jamie away. When was the last time he had shared a meal with a beautiful woman? He often grabbed a bite to eat with Jillian when they were on a tight schedule and she was helping him with some project or another, but that was different. She was practically a little sister. He'd known her forever and didn't think of her in sexual terms.

It was hard to look at Jamie and *not* think of sex. She had a strangely strong effect on him.

One of the worst things about being in prison had

been the lack of female companionship of any kind, and he'd always imagined that the first thing he would do if he regained his freedom was find a beautiful, willing woman and have sex for days on end.

It hadn't happened like that, of course. Once he got out, he'd had to rebuild himself, physically and mentally, before he could even think about bringing another person into the mix. Then he'd had to deal with the deaths of his parents, one right after the other, all while building his fledgling foundation and handling crisis after crisis at Logan Oil & Gas.

Jamie was the first flesh-and-blood woman to arouse him in a very long time.

"I hope you left room for dessert," he found himself saying against his better judgment.

Jamie seemed to rouse herself from the pleasure induced by a superior meal. "Oh, no, I don't have time for that."

Daniel reached for the hardwired phone that was nestled in a stone niche near their table. "Cora, we're ready for dessert," he told Claude's assistant when she answered. "What's on the menu today?"

"Tiramisu," Cora said. "I'll get a couple of slices right down to you."

"Tiramisu," he repeated for Jamie's benefit.

"I really have to go."

"Another few minutes won't—"

"No, I really *have* to go." She was much firmer this time as she scooted her chair out and found her feet.

Daniel was tempted to try to cajole her into staying for dessert. But he risked making her angry, and she'd only just recently lost that tense, mulish expression and begun to speak to him as an intelligent human being, rather than a bug on the sidewalk she'd like to squish.

"I'll show you out, then," he said amicably. He picked up the phone again and pushed the Jillian button—every phone in the house had a Jillian button. After speaking briefly to his assistant, he showed Jamie back through his office where she grabbed her all-but-forgotten briefcase. They continued up the stairs and down the long hall that led to the front door.

"Who are all these people?" Jamie asked, nodding toward the portraits that lined the walls. "Logan ancestors?"

"Good heavens, no. Most of my ancestors were Scottish peasants, not the kind who were immortalized by great artists. My grandfather bought most of these paintings as investments."

"Your grandfather was a self-made man?"

"If you call discovering oil on your little piece of hardscrabble farm *made* and not *lucky.*"

"I imagine it takes a bit more than luck to build an empire the size of this one."

"Some hard work," Daniel agreed. "My father was never home for dinner. Worked himself to an early grave."

"I take it that's not your philosophy."

"Make no mistake, Jamie, I work hard. But I also take care of myself, and I insist my employees do, too. What's the point of working yourself to a frazzle— even for something you care deeply about—if you're not around to appreciate the fruits of your labor?"

"I guess people do it so their children will have the kind of life they didn't," Jamie said, rather philosophically.

"Is that what your father did?"

"Oh, no. My father wanted me to live exactly the same life he did." An edge in her voice suggested disapproval.

"He was a lawyer, too, I take it. A prosecutor?" His research had told him Jamie was born out of wedlock and the father was out of the picture.

She didn't answer, and Daniel thought better of pursuing the subject. They'd arrived in the foyer, and Jillian was there, clipboard in hand as well as a small, white cardboard box, which she handed to Jamie with a brittle smile.

"What's this?"

"Tiramisu. Something to nosh on if you get stuck in traffic again. Daniel didn't want you to miss it. Although our chef, Claude, is French, not Italian, he does an incredible job."

"Thank you," Jamie said uncertainly.

"No, thank you," Daniel said, meaning it. "I know it was an imposition, driving out to River Oaks, but I appreciate you taking the time to meet with me. I believe in the end you'll be glad you did."

She turned to face him, and that mulish expression had returned to her face. "Mr. Logan. Best-case scenario for me is that you've wasted some of my time. Worst case, you make me look like an incompetent fool and possibly cost me my job."

"I hope it won't come to that."

"If you're right, that is exactly what would happen. Believe it or not, I would be willing to accept unemployment if you could prove I'd made such a heinous mistake. But I'm not willing to be made a fool simply because you have the money, and the clout, and the patience to get your way. I will not give in simply to be done with this. I will fight you every step of the way, no matter how good your freaking tiramisu is."

On that note, Jillian opened the front door for her, and Jamie stepped out into the blustery fall day toward her car.

Jillian closed the front door with a bit more force than necessary. "She's a real piece of work."

"I thought she was fantastic! Intelligent, outspoken, passionate about her work…"

"And drop-dead gorgeous," Jillian observed drily. "I don't suppose you're crushing on her, are you?"

"Jillian, please. I'm well out of adolescence. I don't get crushes."

"Whatever you call it, I hope you won't let it get in

the way of what you have to do. Because to free Christopher Gables, you might very well have to *crush* one passionate, overzealous prosecutor."

WHAT JUST HAPPENED BACK THERE?

Jamie's hands actually trembled as she put the car in gear and headed toward the gates that were, even now, opening for her. She'd walked into Daniel Logan's home practically breathing fire, ready to dazzle him with her facts and her smart-ass wit. Instead, she'd found herself ogling a half-naked man, sharing one of the best meals she could remember while the same man wore nothing but a bathrobe, and saying yes to something she never should have agreed to.

Now she was committed to giving Theresa Chavez an audience. And if the woman convincingly claimed to have witnessed someone other than Christopher Gables killing Frank Sissom, Jamie could not, in good conscience, dismiss the woman's statement.

She would have to investigate. She would have to find out if it really was the same woman who discovered the body, then fled, and then determine if the woman was credible.

None of which would change the fact that Christopher Gables's fingerprints, and only his prints, were found on the murder weapon. But if she didn't perform due diligence, Daniel Logan would never leave her alone.

She knew how Project Justice operated, because

quite a few cases prosecuted by her office had been overturned due to the persistence of the foundation's people. Daniel—who believed in this case so strongly that he had taken it on personally—would not give up until he was convinced beyond any reasonable doubt that his client really was guilty.

God, what a nightmare. Winston Chubb, the district attorney, wasn't going to be happy with this turn of events. And he would find a way to blame Jamie for it, she was sure. Winston always managed to grab the credit for anything good that happened, and passed the buck regarding anything bad.

On top of everything else, she could smell the tiramisu, faint threads of chocolate, vanilla and coffee. She ought to just throw the little white box—tied with a satin ribbon, for God's sake—into the first trash can she saw. The dessert was a symbol of everything that had gone wrong with that meeting, including her completely inappropriate physical reaction to the billionaire.

Imagine her, Jamie McNair, attracted to a convicted killer! But she was.

It was hard to visualize Daniel Logan killing anyone. Even knowing the facts, she hadn't felt the least bit uncomfortable alone in his presence, other than having to hammer down her libido.

But then, people had said that about Ted Bundy.

THIRTY MINUTES LATER, Jamie was back into her office and the little white box was empty, damn it.

Her day was shot. A pile of cases sat on her desk—mostly routine plea-bargain requests from defense attorneys. She went through as many as she could, signing off on the reasonable ones, rejecting the more outrageous requests for repeat felons and violent offenders.

She spent an hour returning phone calls, talked to three different detectives regarding a felony assault case, then checked her schedule for the following day.

Jury selection for a drunk hit-and-run case in the morning; three appointments in the afternoon.

With fifteen minutes left of her official workday, Jamie did what she'd known she would do all along. She opened the Gables/Sissom murder file and dug through a mountain of reports until she found the one from the crime lab regarding the evidence they'd processed—bloodstains, fingerprints, the knife and, finally, the victim's clothing.

Most of the details regarding the clothing had to do with bloodstains—including one tiny biological stain on the apron that hadn't belonged to the victim and had remained unidentified. But there was also a list of substances other than blood found on the victim's shirt, which included olive oil, tomato juice, salt—all the things once might expect to find on someone who spent time in a restaurant kitchen.

One finding, though, made Jamie stop: "a black, powdery substance assumed to be from a laser printer or copy machine."

Assumed to be? Since when did crime-scene analysts

assume anything? Probably the restaurant had a printer or copy machine, and since Frank Sissom was one of the owners, she had every reason to believe he'd been in the office and changed a printer cartridge.

But a black, powdery substance could also be metal shavings. Damn it.

She called the guy who'd signed the report, Eddie Goddard. He'd been working at the crime lab since Jamie was in high school, and though he was normally thorough and dependable, he still was not her favorite person. A card-carrying member of the Good Ol' Boys Club, he didn't like women telling him what to do.

"Eddie. I see you're working late like me." It was now well after five.

"I was just heading out, actually. What can I do for you?" He did not sound enthusiastic about adding any tasks to his To Do list.

"I won't stop you from getting home in time for dinner," she promised, hoping to earn brownie points. "But tomorrow morning, I'm going to bring you a piece of clothing from the Frank Sissom case. I need some additional analysis on a certain stain."

"You're joking, right? That case is ancient."

"Wish I was. But I need to shut somebody up before he goes to the press and makes our lives more miserable than they already are. A quick look-see under a microscope will probably do the trick." She hoped.

"Okay, sure," he agreed in monotone.

Tomorrow morning, she would retrieve the actual physical evidence from the police, hand the victim's shirt over to Eddie and pray that Theresa Chavez didn't call.

CHAPTER THREE

"DANIEL, SORRY TO disturb you, but Jamie McNair is on line two."

The four men and two women seated in Daniel's conference room looked surprised by the interruption, and it was no wonder; his staff knew not to disturb him during a Logan Oil & Gas board meeting. The company was largely responsible for maintaining Daniel's personal wealth, and Daniel remained involved in the overall direction and philosophy of the company his grandfather had started.

The meeting was important, but Jamie took priority.

"I have to take this call," Daniel said to the board as he rose. "Shouldn't last more than five minutes."

When Jamie had left his home two days ago, Daniel hadn't been sure how, or even if, she would follow up. So he was a bit surprised and pleased that she'd called him.

He stepped down the hall and into his private office, then picked up the phone.

"Jamie. Good to hear from you."

"Mr. Logan."

Damn, she didn't sound nearly as warm as he'd hoped. "Did Theresa get in touch with you?" He already knew she had; he'd personally seen to it. He'd even hired a car and driver to take her to the district attorney's office for an interview.

"She did. And I'll be honest with you, she piqued my interest."

"Then you'll reopen the case," he said confidently.

"Don't get your hopes up. She seemed genuine, but I still haven't verified she was at the scene of the crime. For all I know, she's an actress you hired."

Daniel bit his tongue to stifle a snide retort. After spending six years hitting brick wall after brick wall trying to overturn his own conviction, he shouldn't be a bit surprised by Jamie's attitude.

"I can provide the documentation you need—"

"I'll provide my own, thanks very much. And if I find out she's lying, I'll personally see to it she's prosecuted. And if I find you paid her to lie, I'll prosecute you."

Daniel was livid. He was so tired of this attitude. Of course, the Harris County D.A.'s office would be doubly motivated to prevent another overturned conviction; Project Justice had recently gained freedom for a mobster's son convicted of killing his girlfriend, and the case had caused some major embarrassment for the D.A.

"It sounds as if you simply don't like me very much. Are you going to let personal feelings stand in the way of justice?"

"Please stop being so simplistic. I'm convinced I did a good job convicting Christopher Gables. Naturally, it's going to take a solid argument to persuade me I made a mistake."

"We're talking about a man's life here."

"Yes, the life of Frank Sissom, Gables's victim. Do you have anything else to show me? If so, bring it on."

"What about that unidentified DNA?"

"If you have a theory about where it came from—or any other evidence—I'm willing to talk. Contrary to what you might believe, I do not have a closed mind. In fact, I'm having one of our evidence analysts reexamine Frank Sissom's apron."

"Really?" She'd succeeded in surprising him.

"I should have results tomorrow."

"Then by all means, we should talk again. When can you get here? I can free up my schedule anytime—"

"I'm glad to hear that, because mine is packed. I can spare you an hour tomorrow afternoon or Monday morning, here at my office."

Daniel's heart clutched, and he forced himself to breathe deeply. "I can't possibly drive downtown."

"Afraid you'd miss your afternoon massage? Exactly how serious are you about wanting to free your client? I disrupted my whole schedule to drive to River Oaks. If you want my cooperation, you can meet me halfway. Besides, we might need to talk to people in the crime lab or the investigating officers involved in the case—all of whom can be found downtown."

"I can send one of my best people." And admit to his staff—already skeptical—that he was not up to handling a case on his own. That would be a bitter pill to swallow.

"Okay. Your assistant can meet with my assistant."

Now she was playing hardball. "Ms. McNair. Jamie. This matter is too serious for us to play games."

"Don't talk to me about games. You're the one who made me cool my heels while you got your massage and sent me home with tiramisu, trying to butter me up."

Maybe she had a point. "Did you like it, by the way? Chef Claude is a genius."

"That is immaterial. I've got a lot on my plate and I really don't have time to chase after every hard-luck and if-only story I hear. You believe he's innocent? Fair enough. Show me the commitment that says you mean it. I'm willing to listen, but I'm not going to deal with layer upon layer of assistants and bodyguards. You started this, and I think you should be the one to finish it. Personally."

His awareness of her primed his body for action, even over the phone. She wanted to deal with him personally, did she? Her reasons sounded plausible, but he didn't completely buy them. Perhaps she wanted to see more of him, just as he wanted to see more of her. He would have been pleased, if not for the massive logistic problem her ultimatum caused.

"What's it going to be?" she prompted. "I'm due in court in ten minutes."

"Name your time," he finally said. "I'll be there, so long as you keep our meeting discreet. Being out in public can cause difficulties for me."

"Believe me, I'm as anxious as you to keep this thing under wraps. Two o'clock tomorrow? I can reserve the conference room."

"I'll be there." Come hell or high water. He hadn't heard any flooding forecasts for South Texas, but hell was a definite possibility.

The board meeting broke up at close to noon. After seeing everyone out to their cars, Jillian returned to Daniel's office to go over his afternoon schedule.

"It's nice poolside, if you'd like to take your lunch there. You haven't breathed any fresh air in a couple of days."

He resisted the urge to remind Jillian that the filtered air in his home was nine times cleaner than the smog-infused air of Houston. "Good suggestion." Dirty air or not, he liked sitting outside when he could, looking out over his swimming pool and listening to birds and wind in the trees. It helped him think, and he had a lot of thinking to do. And it reminded him he was a free man.

"Also, Jillian, please have the limo ready tomorrow at 1:30—no, 1:15. I'm going downtown to meet with Jamie McNair… What?"

The unflappable Jillian's mouth gaped open. "You're going downtown?" she repeated.

"Yes. Maybe not in the limo, I don't want to draw attention. The Bentley might be better."

"You are going downtown," she said again.

"It's the Christopher Gables case. Ms. McNair is willing to talk, which is frankly more than I expected at this stage."

"But...*you're* going to a meeting? Personally?"

"Jillian, have you gone hard of hearing? I'm perfectly capable of attending a meeting off-site. I'll admit, I usually choose not to, but this is important."

"With all due respect, sir, you haven't left the estate in three years."

That stopped him. "Three— Oh, surely you're mistaken."

"Your grandmother's funeral in Miami. October 3, two thousand—"

"It doesn't matter. I'm going. I have to go."

Jillian's face softened. "Do you want me to come with you?"

The tightness in his chest eased slightly as he pictured Jillian sitting next to him, dealing with pesky details. But when he pictured himself meeting with Jamie, he saw the two of them alone.

Hell, he didn't need Jillian to hover and fuss over him. He could handle this mission on his own. He had taken on the responsibility of being Christopher Gables's champion, and he needed to see it through.

"No, thank you, Jillian. I'll bring Randall for security. That should be sufficient."

Jillian looked as if she wanted to argue, but in the end she nodded her head and turned. "Yes, sir."

THE FOLLOWING DAY, Daniel sucked up a monumental case of nerves and strode to his limo parked in the driveway. He'd opted for the larger, more ostentatious car after all; it seemed safer.

He had a briefcase full of information about the Sissom/Gables case as well as the Andreas Musto murder—the parallels between the two cases simply could not be coincidence. He'd even drawn up a chart, with graphics, showing similarities. And if there was a remote chance that he could find the person who'd stolen six years of his life…

Daniel wasn't a violent man, as his lawyers had so tirelessly reminded the jury. But if he ever came face-to-face with the man who'd framed him, he could easily kill with his bare hands. That thought had provided comfort during many sleepless nights.

His special-order Mercedes limousine was familiar and comforting, and he breathed in the scent of well-tended leather. But the car must be at least four years old now.

"Randall," he said just before his driver and body-guard closed his door, "order a new limousine."

"Is something wrong with the car?" Randall asked, concerned. He was the one who insisted on personally keeping the vehicle in perfect condition, mechanically and cosmetically.

"No, it's just time." Keeping up appearances didn't really matter much to him, but others depended on his maintaining a certain image. The slightest show of weakness—financial or otherwise—could give rise to rumors that could affect Logan Oil & Gas stock prices, and the well-being of countless investors who'd risked their retirement to his care.

Moments later, the car eased down the driveway and the wrought-iron gates opened noiselessly.

And Daniel felt sick to his stomach.

The car was as safe as any presidential limo, with triple-thick steel doors and bulletproof tinted glass. Randall was a former Secret Service agent, an expert in every sort of bodyguard skill on the planet, including evasive driving, marksmanship and hand-to-hand combat. But that didn't stop Daniel from envisioning everything that could go wrong—car accidents, breakdown, traffic snarls, Randall suddenly falling ill...

Daniel told himself it was because he was nervous about meeting Jamie. She'd opened the door a crack; if he was late, she might slam it shut again, making his job more difficult. But the truth was, he just wanted to turn around. Behind the brick wall and iron gates, Daniel dictated everything that happened around him.

Away from that cocoon, anything could happen.

What had gone wrong with him? He'd once loved adventure. He'd traveled, embarked on business ventures, tried every sport he could manage. He'd climbed mountains, dated movie stars and earned a business degree from Harvard.

Now, just leaving the house took a monumental dose of courage.

Yes, being falsely accused of a murder he didn't commit, then going through the trial and six years of incarceration on death row, was bound to change a man. Once he'd been freed, he'd come home and, for the first time in a very long time, he'd felt safe and loved.

But even back then, he hadn't been housebound. He'd made periodic trips to Logan Oil and to Project Justice after his father's death to keep things running. He'd attended funerals and visited doctors.

But the past few years he'd ventured forth less and less as the people he'd hired to run his empire had competently taken over.

I'm fine, damn it.

There was nothing wrong with how he'd chosen to live. After what he'd been through—having a good chunk of his youth stolen away—he ought to be allowed to enjoy his every hour of freedom on his own terms. Thanks to his father and grandfather, plus a few smart decisions he'd made, he had the money to do that, and he refused to feel guilty about it.

Focus on the prize, he told himself. He had to think about Christopher. Succeeding with his mission to find justice for Christopher meant giving a man back his life, and Daniel knew what a huge gift that was. Succeeding also meant more favorable publicity for Project Justice, which was important to all those other men and women the foundation could help.

Then there was the little matter of showing smug Jamie she didn't know everything. Somehow, though, that thought didn't fill him with the pleasure he thought it would.

Finally, there was the satisfaction vengeance would bring.

Daniel cracked a tinted window, immediately aware of how different the breeze from outside felt. It smelled wild. Unsafe.

"Nice day for a drive," Randall said. Daniel had left the glass partition open. "Sometimes I miss the old days, just you and me out and about in the Jaguar."

"We were a pair, weren't we? Tearing through town like we didn't have a care in the world." That was back when Daniel thought he was invincible.

The bodyguard's presence reassured Daniel. Randall was the best—discreet and potentially deadly. He looked ordinary enough, harmless even with his light brown skin, round face and close-cropped, salt-and-pepper hair.

But appearances could be deceiving.

Daniel considered Randall a friend. He was good company—educated, intelligent, funny. And they'd once spent countless hours together.

But they'd had little face-to-face contact in recent years.

Daniel spent the short drive toward downtown looking over papers in his briefcase, information he already knew by heart. He had an almost photographic memory. But he wanted to have answers right at hand for any questions Jamie might pose—and the hard data to back him up.

Jamie. Seeing her again was worth all this trouble. She was the first person in a very long time to challenge him—or excite him. Though of course he couldn't know her on anything but a professional level, the undeniable electricity that charged the air around them when they were in the same room added an element of interest to this case.

Daniel didn't "date." He could not envision himself in a real romantic relationship. Sharing with anyone the world he'd so carefully crafted would ruin it. But that didn't stop him from the occasional fantasy, and lately Jamie McNair had taken a starring role in his daydreams. He'd also lost a bit of sleep over her, as she'd appeared in his night dreams, too.

He'd best not get too attached to his fantasy. When he put the prosecutor in her place, firmly convinced she wasn't infallible, she wouldn't gratefully fall into his arms.

Traffic was light, and soon they were wending through downtown streets. Crowded. Noisy.

Abruptly, Daniel shut his window, sealing the noise outside. But that didn't stop the panic that suddenly rose in his chest.

He could stop now. Turn around. Cancel the meeting,

hand the whole thing over to Ford or Raleigh, his top lieutenants. There was time. Although Christopher's appeals had run out, his execution hadn't yet been scheduled.

The urge to run was so strong, it made Daniel lightheaded.

"Do you know the suite number of Ms. McNair's office?" Randall asked.

Daniel turned to Jillian, realized she wasn't there, and his panic increased. "I wrote it down somewhere... Hell." It was a simple detail, but his mind was suddenly blank. "I'll look it up."

He checked his schedule on his phone. Yes, there it was, on the sixth floor.

He cast his mind ahead to the coming meeting with Jamie, but now he had trouble visualizing it. Was that because he was about to enter an unknown building with unfamiliar elevators and strangers within inches of him? Perhaps.

Or maybe it was the unpredictable woman herself. For the first time in a long time, he would not be in control of every detail around him. It was both exciting and terrifying.

He shook his head. Billions of people could walk into a strange building without thinking twice. He was being ridiculous. If Jamie perceived any nervousness or weakness, she could gain an advantage. Especially on her home turf.

As they turned onto Franklin Street, Daniel couldn't

believe his eyes. Three TV news vans, bristling with antennae and satellite dishes, were parked at odd angles in front of the Harris County Criminal Justice Center. Reporters with microphones and cameramen and -women crawled the sidewalks and steps to the contemporary skyscraper, along with a crowd of at least a hundred curious onlookers.

The limo pulled to a stop, and lots of heads turned to gawk. Cameras swiveled in Daniel's direction.

"What the hell...?" If Jamie had engineered this welcome wagon, he would wring her neck. Hadn't he emphasized how important privacy and discretion were? Had she done this to deliberately sabotage his efforts?

"Any idea what's going on?" Randall asked.

"None." He quickly dialed in the internet on his phone and checked the local headlines. "Ah. Judge John Harlow was caught in the backseat of his car with a fifteen-year-old. Story broke this morning."

"You can't get out here," Randall said firmly. "If the press gets wind that you're out and about, it'll ruin any chance you have of conducting normal business."

"Is it really a front-page story? I mean, come on."

"Yes, Daniel. You driving downtown to meet with a prosecutor about Christopher Gables would be front-page material."

Daniel thought he had a pretty good grip on the media and their opinion of him. After all, he watched every news channel all day in his office. Did he have a blind spot where he, personally, was concerned?

More important, what was he going to do now? He wished he'd brought Jillian. She could contact Jamie, smooth things over, reschedule the meeting—

Hell, what was he thinking? He could call Jamie himself. He had the fanciest cell phone on the planet, which Jillian programmed with any number he might need.

Moments later he was dialing Jamie's direct number, and a rush of sweet anticipation coursed through him as he waited for her to answer.

JAMIE WAS AS PREPARED for her meeting with Daniel Logan as she could be. She had reserved the conference room, and had even sprung for a snack tray from the deli around the corner out of her own pocket. Daniel had fed her lavishly, so she felt obligated to at least see that he didn't go hungry while on her turf.

Frankly, she was surprised—and flush with inappropriate pleasure—that he had agreed to her terms. As she assembled her stack of papers she intended to present, she couldn't deny a certain eagerness. But behind it was a dark cloud of impending doom she couldn't shake.

If Daniel succeeded in his quest, her job was in danger. Certainly her chances of rising to any level of prominence in the district attorney's office would be quashed. Winston Chubb had been livid when she'd told him what Daniel Logan was up to. Though he feared the man, Chubb had instructed her to neutralize Logan and his do-gooder efforts using any means at her disposal.

Any means.

As she returned to her desk to check messages one last time before the meeting, the phone rang. The number on caller ID was blocked and she considered letting it go to voice mail. But at the last minute she picked it up. If it was Daniel, telling her he was delayed, she would politely remind him she couldn't rearrange her schedule—just as he'd done to her.

"McNair." Her voice came out a bit sharper than she'd intended.

"It's Daniel. I'm in front of your building now, but I'm trapped. There's a media frenzy going on out here, and if I step out of my car I'll become a part of the uproar."

"Oh, for the love of—" She tried mightily to hold on to her patience as she moved to the window and looked down. From her sixth-floor office she had a perfect view of the front entrance, and it was exactly as Daniel had described.

"It's the Judge Harlow thing, I imagine," Daniel said.

Jamie sighed in frustration. She hadn't yet read her newspaper today, but she'd heard about the judge. The whole office buzzed with the news. Just what the city needed, another scandal.

"Is there a back entrance?" Daniel asked.

"I'm afraid not. With our heightened security, everyone has to come and go through the front doors. You'll just have to cope."

"I can't." His voice held a note of panic. "It's highly

unlikely I would make it into the building unobserved. And I don't think either of us wants to see our business splashed on the front page until we're ready."

He did have a point. "What do you suggest? My time is extremely limited. I'm awaiting a jury verdict, and I could be called back into court at any minute."

"We can meet in my car. There's a big backseat—it's private, it's roomy and very secure."

Jamie didn't like it. Not at all. Was he simply manipulating her, forcing her to abandon her plans and conduct the meeting on his turf—again?

But she couldn't deny that a security problem existed. That crowd outside looked hungry, and if they couldn't get a glimpse of the judge or at least get a statement from someone in Public Relations about the situation, they would take what they could get.

And they would have a heyday with the juicy combination of Daniel Logan trying to free Christopher Gables. They would grab on to the surface similarities between the cases, and she would have to spend all of her time chasing down rumors and denying, denying, denying.

"All right, we can meet in your car," she said, barely able to part her jaws to get the words out. "Give me a few minutes to gather my materials." And her wits.

She was about to get in the backseat of a car with a man who had the ability to short-circuit her rational mind and possibly tank her whole career.

"Thank you," he said, sounding like he meant it. His

relief was almost palpable. "It's the black Mercedes limo parked near the corner."

Five minutes later, she was wending her way past reporters and cameras on the walkway leading from the criminal justice building to the street. Despite her efforts to appear insignificant and ignorant, one reporter jumped into her path and stuck a microphone in her face.

"Ms. McNair, can you comment on the situation with Judge—"

"Even if I knew anything, which I don't, I wouldn't comment. Excuse me." She stepped around the microphone, hoping the reporter holding it would focus on someone else.

A few more steps, and she reached the longest, blackest, shiniest vehicle she'd ever seen. A uniformed driver popped out to open the back door and she slid in as quickly as possible, praying no one noticed. The only time she'd been at the center of media attention—during the Christopher Gables trial—she hadn't liked it. It was something she needed to get comfortable with, though, if she wanted to advance in her chosen profession.

Jamie kept her eyes focused down on herself as she smoothed her skirt and gathered her thoughts. Only then did she look up and face Daniel Logan.

At least he had clothes on this time. But the effect of Daniel in a well-tailored gray suit and silk tie was no less devastating to her hormones. Her heart gave a little jump, and she sucked in her breath.

He held out his hand. "Jamie. Sorry for the inconvenience."

She took his hand. "Daniel. Thank you for coming."

It was the first time she'd called him by his given name. She'd been avoiding it, because it seemed a bit too chummy. Too intimate, given their adversarial relationship.

But it seemed positively Victorian to keep calling him Mr. Logan.

As soon as she could do so politely, she eased her hand away from the warmth of his. His handshake absolutely oozed confidence. How did he do that? And what did hers communicate? Shivering nerves?

"How was the traffic?" she asked, because that was what everyone in Houston asked first thing in any meeting.

"I wasn't really paying attention," he admitted. "I was going over my notes. But I guess it was okay. We got here quickly."

Of course he didn't have to concern himself with mundane matters like traffic. He had a chauffeur and a limousine the size of a battleship. She tried to imagine living like him—hot and cold running servants, mostly hot from what she'd seen—a three-story mansion, polo ponies and tennis courts. She couldn't even wrap her mind around it. She couldn't imagine what it would be like to not work like a dog every day, watch her spending, save for retirement.

She resented the ease of his life. Yeah, six years on death row wouldn't have been a picnic. But he'd been convicted of murder. And here he was, flaunting his wealth and dabbling in "charitable" work, helping others like himself escape retribution for their crimes.

"So," she said crisply, imagining a clear shell around her that would make her immune to the handsome billionaire's physical proximity. "The driver can't hear us, can he?" She glanced at the glass partition that separated the driver from the passenger seating.

"Not a word. We could scream at the tops of our lungs and he wouldn't hear us."

That thought didn't particularly cheer her.

"Yes, well. Since I called this meeting, and we have limited time, let's get started."

"All right. Tell me about Theresa."

That was a good place to start. "She was credible. Sincere. My investigation leaves me certain she is the same Theresa who made the 9-1-1 call, bringing the police to El Toreador. And her statement about seeing a stranger in the restaurant kitchen sounds plausible."

"Only plausible? You don't think it rings with truth?"

"Plausible," she said firmly.

Daniel's eyes almost twinkled as he listened attentively with his whole body. She liked that about him, even if she disapproved of everything else. So many people—men especially—might appear to be listening, but they were actually waiting for their turn to speak.

"I'm very glad to hear you say that," he said. "Can you show her mug shots? Have her work with a sketch artist? I have an artist on call for Project Justice that does excellent work."

Now came the hard part. "As I've explained before, one eyewitness statement, delivered all these years after the crime, will not trump the physical evidence. All Theresa gave me was a vague description. She saw an unfamiliar man in the kitchen talking to the victim. Minutes later, as she was bussing tables, she heard a loud crash in the kitchen and went to investigate. She found the victim dead."

"But she gave *some* description, right? Male Caucasian in his thirties, medium build..."

"Wearing a baseball cap, so she couldn't even get a hair color. It's too general."

"But she told you it was positively *not* Christopher Gables. Correct?"

"Yes," Jamie admitted. "But if we press her for details at this point...well, it's easy for the mind to play tricks. Her subconscious could provide details just to please me."

Daniel opened his mouth to object, but she cut him off.

"Not that she would deceive me on purpose, but memory is a strange and unreliable beast. Considering your experience with Project Justice, I'm sure you understand that."

Daniel seemed to deflate slightly. "Still, it seems

likely to me that if this stranger was the last person seen talking to Frank before he died, he is a more probable suspect than Christopher."

"Except that his prints weren't found on the murder weapon."

Daniel pressed his lips together, and Jamie tasted victory. At last, she just might have convinced him he was on a fool's errand.

She tried to press her advantage. "I brought the case file with me. I'm ready to go step-by-step through the thinking process that led me to prosecute this case."

"I'd like that."

Jamie opened her briefcase just as her phone rang. It was rude to take a call during a meeting, but she was still waiting for that verdict.

"I'm sorry, this might be important." She quickly looked at the caller ID. "Oh. You may actually be interested in this." It was Eddie, the evidence tech whom she'd bullied into taking another look at Frank Sissom's clothing. "Yes, Eddie?"

"I got the results on those stains. Put it through the spectrometer. It's not toner powder at all."

Her stomach sank. *Let it be dirt. Charcoal. Cigarette ash.* "Well, what is it?"

"Very fine metal filings. Ferrous."

This could not be happening to her. Metal filings? As in exactly what Daniel had predicted she would find?

"Thanks, Eddie, I'll get back to you."

"Well?" Daniel said. Then his face softened. "Jamie,

what's wrong? You're pale. Did he say something to upset you?"

Her lips felt suddenly cold, and she could barely form the words. "You said something about a s-serial killer?"

CHAPTER FOUR

"WHO WAS THAT ON THE PHONE?" Daniel asked sharply. Whoever it was, he'd sure said something to shake up Jamie.

"My evidence tech, the one reexamining Frank Sissom's clothes. He found something no one else did—very fine metal shavings."

Daniel could hardly believe what he was hearing. His long shot had paid off. "Jamie, this is huge. Do you realize what this means?" In his exuberance, he threw his arms around the lawyer and hugged her. Finally, someone had listened to him about those damn metal shavings.

"Um, do you always get this happy at the prospect of helping a client?"

Suddenly self-conscious, he released her and scooted back a few inches on the enormous bench seat. "Sorry." Had he been out of the social scene so long, he'd forgotten how to behave appropriately with someone he barely knew?

Only, he felt as if he knew her. Over the past twenty-four hours, he had delved deeply into Jamie McNair's background, and his admiration for her had only grown.

Her roots had come from anything but privilege. Her single mother had raised her in a one-bedroom apartment with a series of low-paying jobs. Her father was completely absent—Daniel hadn't even been able to learn his identity.

Yet Jamie had gotten herself an education with a lot of hard work, scholarships and student loans. Still not rolling in dough, judging from her off-the-rack plum-colored suit and a pair of slightly scuffed black pumps—recently polished, but in need of new soles.

Not that she didn't look stunning in that color. She would look stunning in just about anything.

Daniel forced himself to focus. "You don't share my optimism, I take it."

"Frankly, I'm too shocked to know what I feel. The black, powdery substance on Frank Sissom's shirt was written off as copier or printer toner. No one ever questioned it or analyzed it until now. It didn't seem relevant."

"I've learned it's those tiny, overlooked elements that can make or break a case. So, are we on the same page now? Same offender?"

"It warrants looking into," she said with some degree of resignation. "One thing I can't help but notice—Frank Sissom was murdered a scant two months after you were released from prison. If we have a serial offender, who's to say it isn't you?"

Daniel felt a prickling of fear. He'd never even considered that he could become a suspect. But he grabbed a bottled water and took a sip to relieve his suddenly dry mouth.

"Why would I push to exonerate Christopher and find the real murderer, if the real murderer was me?" he asked sensibly.

She shrugged. "I'll put that possibility on the back burner. For now. But that leaves me with Gables as a two-time murderer."

Daniel curbed his impatience. "Gables was a college kid at the time of the first crime."

"College kids are adults, perfectly capable of homicide."

One inch at a time. Daniel had more now than he did last time he'd met with Jamie. He just had to keep building.

"Back to the metal shavings. Was your guy able to distinguish the type of metal, or where it might have come from?"

"Well, it's ferrous, which means iron or nickel, or an alloy of either. We haven't gotten beyond that yet. The type of close analysis you're talking about takes time... and money."

"I'll give you the name of a lab. They do photochemical spectography, which can give us the exact— What?"

Her expression was closed again, guarded. "It's not

just a question of time or money. My boss is going to throw a fit."

"Does he have to know?"

"Of course he does! If you're right, if Christopher Gables was involved in two murders—"

"Wait. Stop right there. You can't seriously think Gables is a serial killer."

"How can you know it's *not* Gables? Look at it from my perspective, Daniel. I am as sure as I've ever been that Christopher Gables committed the murder of Frank Sissom. You can't argue away those fingerprints. If trace evidence links this murder to another, then Christopher might well be involved in the previous murder, as well. It only makes sense."

It made no sense at all.

"Would you like me to give you an explanation for the fingerprints?" Daniel asked.

"Oh, this I've got to hear."

Daniel had given this a lot of thought. Because, unlike Jamie, he knew beyond any shadow of a doubt that he hadn't killed anyone, yet his prints had been found on a murder weapon.

"Christopher used the knife for something else— hours, days, even months prior to the murder. So long as no one else touches the knife, the prints remain intact.

"The real murderer then uses an identical knife to commit the crime. Wearing gloves, he smears some blood on the knife bearing Christopher's prints and places it near the body. Voilà, a perfect frame-up."

"The medical examiner matched the knife to the wound," she argued.

Daniel opened his briefcase, rifled through it until he came up with a page of the trial transcript with some testimony highlighted in yellow.

"'The wound on Mr. Sissom's neck is consistent with a Messermeister Meridian Elite eight-inch chef's knife—the knife found near his body.' Do you recognize that testimony, Jamie?"

She closed her eyes for a moment. "Yes."

"'…is consistent with…' doesn't mean the same as 'exact match,' does it?"

"Please, I'm not on trial here. You've made your point. The murder could have been committed with an identical knife."

"You have no idea how many nights I lie awake, thinking about how my prints ended up on a murder weapon. I had no conscious memory of using the knife that killed my partner. I'm not a chef, and I spent little time in the kitchen."

"So how do you explain it?"

"I tried to think of the things I might use a knife for. And here's what I came up with. I might have used a knife to open a package. Not the day of the murder, but perhaps weeks earlier. I had a penknife I kept in my pocket for such things, because the restaurant received packages all the time. But I could have mislaid it and picked up whatever was handy."

Daniel could almost see the gears turning in Jamie's head as she mulled over his theory.

"Christopher wasn't a chef, either," she finally said. "Our theory was that Christopher confronted Frank in the kitchen, knowing ahead of time he would have his choice of murder weapons."

"I'd like to talk to him," Daniel said. "See if he has any memory of touching that knife for an innocent purpose."

"I can answer that for you. He said he used it to cut up an apple for lunch that day. Which was an obvious lie, because he always ate something off the menu for his lunch, and at least three witnesses saw him eating fajitas."

"It was a lie, I'll grant you that. Probably concocted on the spur of the moment out of fear and desperation. Have you ever been interrogated, Jamie?"

"No, but I've witnessed many police interviews and watched loads of video."

"That's not the same. Until you're locked in that room with a couple of mean-eyed cops, pointing fingers at you, shouting at you, playing head games with you—you have no idea what it's like. You are tempted to say anything, no matter how untrue, just to get those guys to leave you alone."

"Did you?" Jamie asked, not without compassion.

"I didn't. But I was still secure in the belief that my father and his influence and money would straighten everything out. Christopher didn't have that to fall back on.

"I submit that he told that lie because he was terrified. And his lawyer coached him to continue the lie rather than admit to it."

Jamie digested the story some more.

Daniel gave her a few moments of silence before he pressed his argument. "Raleigh, our chief legal counsel, has put in the paperwork for a face-to-face interview with Christopher. I'd like you to go with her to the prison."

"Raleigh? Why not you?"

"Prison officials have to grant an interview for a death-row inmate with his attorney of record. I'm not an attorney."

"Daniel, I know how Project Justice operates. Your people conduct interviews with prisoners on death row all the time, often without an attorney present."

"It wouldn't work this time."

"I submit," she said, reflecting his own verbiage back to him, "that you are not the best person to argue on Christopher's behalf. Not only are you seriously biased because of the similarities between the crimes, but your high profile—by your own admission—makes it difficult for you to move about comfortably in public situations.

"So why don't you assign this case to one of your people. Full-time. It will be easier on everyone."

"My 'serious bias,' as you put it, makes me uniquely

qualified to fight passionately for Christopher's freedom."

"Then don't you think you're the best one to interview him?"

She was right. And yet...the thought of walking into that prison—the very same prison where Daniel had been incarcerated—was abhorrent to him.

"If I agree, will you go with me? Because, as the prosecutor of this case, you also are uniquely qualified to shoot down any half-baked theories. You know what will and won't fly in a courtroom before a judge."

"I'll have to clear it with my boss."

And she'd already told him: her boss hated the idea of reopening this case.

"I'll set something up for next week. That should give you a chance to clear your schedule."

"I'll send the metal shavings for further analysis. What's the name of your lab?"

"PrakTech Laboratories. They're certified by the county, so that shouldn't be a problem. Of course, Project Justice will pick up the bill."

She shook her head, firmed her lips. "I can't believe I'm doing this. I can't believe I've let you talk me into this. In the end, I'll probably trash my career, and for what? Christopher Gables isn't going to walk unless another suspect turns himself in and confesses."

He felt for her. He really did. "You're doing this because a man's life is at stake. You're a good person, and you don't like the thought of prosecuting an innocent man any more than I do."

"Or maybe you're just one persuasive man."

"That, too." He smiled at her for the first time since she'd gotten in the car, and she smiled back.

"I *will* be checking into Christopher Gables's whereabouts at the time of the Andreas Musto murder."

"You would be remiss in your duties if you didn't. Jamie...I want you to know that I'm grateful."

"Because you've backed me into a corner?"

"For doing the right thing. The man who prosecuted my case—Chet Dotie, as I'm sure you know—he stonewalled every effort I made to exonerate myself. He considered my effort a personal affront, and he threw every barrier into my path he could think of, ethical or not."

"I'm sure it looked that way..." She trailed off and looked away, less composed, suddenly. "Prosecutors invest a lot of time and money into an important case. I mean, it's not just about that. Most of them believe... they fight passionately..."

"Dotie didn't believe in it, though," Daniel informed her. "He looked me straight in the eye and told me he didn't care if I'd done it or not, he wasn't going to let some snot-nosed rich kid get out of jail just because his daddy had money."

Jamie's eyebrows shot up and her nostrils flared.

"I'm not telling you this simply to malign one of your own. It's just that the contrast of your open mind is refreshing."

She didn't seem to appreciate the compliment. "We'll see how refreshed you feel when this is all over." Her phone rang, and she answered it without apology this time. "McNair…okay, on my way."

"Verdict's in?"

"I assume I'll hear from you when you have new information."

"And I assume the same."

She shot out of his car like the hounds of hell were chasing her. A few enterprising reporters tried to thwart her progress, but she put her briefcase in front of her like a battering ram and they got out of her way.

He didn't blame them. She seemed soft and sweet sometimes, but then she could turn around and breathe fire at him. The contrast was interesting.

She was interesting. The reporters eyeing his limo were just plain scary. Daniel opened the glass partition. "Let's get out of here."

"You got it."

AS SHE PRACTICALLY SPRINTED UP the stairs toward the justice center, Jamie felt like she couldn't get enough air. Those things he'd said about her father—were they true? Or had he just made up a story to manipulate her emotions?

Daniel might be manipulative, but she hadn't caught him in a lie yet. What little she'd read about his arrest and trial indicated that his story had never changed.

He hadn't made up anything to explain away facts, as Christopher had.

Which left her wondering—was her father not the man she believed he'd been?

She and Chet Dotie had never enjoyed a warm relationship. Although she'd always known his name, her mother had forbid mention of it and had refused to allow her daughter any contact with the man who had sired her.

Apparently her father had sent money from time to time. Although he'd never made any concerted effort to see his daughter, he hadn't completely forgotten her.

That knowledge had led her to seek him out when she was in college, when her mother couldn't stop her. He'd been surprised, confused and not altogether welcoming of her intrusion into his life. But gradually he'd come around when he realized she wasn't going to publicize their relationship and possibly taint his reputation.

He started taking a keen interest in her studies, even paying her tuition on occasion, provided she took the classes he specified. Though she'd been drawn to art and literature, he had pointed out to her that she couldn't afford that indulgence. She needed a career that would provide a solid, regular income. Law school it was. Period.

She had bristled at his high-handedness at first, but she'd soon discovered she was well suited to the legal profession and had settled in to be the best law student she could be.

Chet took for granted her good grades and the prestigious internship she'd earned. She'd thought he was reserving his praise for when she graduated. But then he died suddenly, just before she got her juris doctorate.

She could have gone into private practice, but she'd wanted to follow in his footsteps. Prosecuting crimes had seemed noble. Her father had been well respected, and she thought it a worthy goal to emulate him.

Had it all been a lie? The thought of him telling a man on death row that he didn't care about guilt or innocence turned her stomach.

She should have told Daniel that Chet was her father. But such an emotional bombshell would likely derail the tenuous alliance they'd formed. She needed to stay on friendly terms with him, she reasoned. If this "serial killer" thing panned out, she wanted some say in how the situation was handled.

If Christopher Gables had killed before, and she broke the news, it would be a feather in her cap that she'd been the one to send him to prison.

If, on the other hand, the killings were linked and someone other than Christopher was responsible… No, she didn't want to think about that. It couldn't be true. Daniel had spun a pretty story about the knife and the fingerprints, but it was improbable at best, like something out of an Agatha Christie novel.

She had to stop allowing him to get through her defenses!

Jamie operated on automatic pilot as the verdict for

her drunk-driving case was announced. Guilty. Judge sentenced the defendant to five years. She considered that a victory.

Next stop: the D.A.'s office. Her heart thudded inside her chest as she contemplated how Winston Chubb would take the latest developments she and Daniel had just discussed. The first time she'd brought up the Gables case, he'd nearly blown a gasket.

Winston's admin squeezed her in between appointments. When Jamie tapped on his door, he beckoned her inside with no welcoming smile.

Winston Chubb was tall, angular, almost emaciated, an image that didn't jibe with his name at all. He had sparse black hair and deep-set, probing eyes. He scared the hell out of people in the courtroom.

"Please tell me you got a guilty verdict with the Mosely case," he said.

"Yes. He got five years."

"Okay, then. Good job. Why are you here?"

He didn't waste words, this guy.

"It's the Christopher Gables case."

His face turned to thunder. "Thought I told you to leave that one alone."

"I'd like to. But the witness I told you about was credible. And some evidence has been reanalyzed—"

"Who authorized that?"

He was trying to intimidate her, and she refused to let him. "I did," she said boldly. "I was curious. It turns out the Gables case might be linked to another, earlier murder. The, um, Andreas Musto case."

Winston's bushy eyebrows flew up. "Are you joking?"

"I wouldn't joke about something like this. The surface similarities are enough to intrigue me."

"Please, Jamie, let it drop. When I sent you to talk to Logan, I assumed you would quietly talk him out of this nonsense. I can't afford another scandal. I'm still taking crap from the Anthony Simonetti case. And you—your career is really taking off. You can't afford it, either." This last, he delivered as a warning.

"I feel we don't have a choice. Daniel Logan has made it his personal mission to free Christopher Gables."

"Free him? I thought you said Gables was a possible two-time offender, not that he might be innocent."

"Mr. Logan and I have a difference of opinion as to what the new evidence means. I feel it's important to pursue this so we'll know the truth."

"The truth? God, Jamie, surely you're not that naive. There's no room for truth in the court system, only different interpretations of events and evidence."

Did he really believe that? Was she the only lawyer left who cared about true guilt or innocence?

"If we drop the ball, Logan's going to put his own spin on this. And it won't be pretty."

"Read my lips, Jamie. No. My budget has been cut to the bone, and you know as well as I do every assistant D.A. in this office is overworked. I can't have you gallivanting around on some fool's errand, trying to scare up evidence that will convict a man who's already in jail or exonerate one who's already been pardoned."

"And what if we convicted the wrong man?" she asked. "We can't let Christopher Gables be executed if it's possible we got things wrong."

"If you help Daniel Logan spin the evidence that way, it would be a very, *very* bad development for everyone involved."

Not for Christopher.

It would be easy for Jamie to slink out of her boss's office and tell Daniel she was sorry, but she couldn't cooperate with him anymore unless she wanted to lose her job.

But that was a coward's way out.

"Jamie. You're one of my brightest stars. Keep your nose clean, get a few more showy convictions and in a couple more years you might be sitting in this chair."

"Me? District attorney?" She almost fell over.

"Why not you? You're attractive, smart, hard as an unripe pumpkin and you get the job done. I'm not running for reelection. Someone has to replace me, and it might as well be you."

Winston made a shooing gesture with his hands. "Go, Jamie. Earn your paycheck. And don't lead with your heart."

Dazed, Jamie backed out of the office and closed the door. District attorney? She didn't appreciate that he'd mentioned her looks first, or that he'd compared her to a vegetable, but if he really meant what he'd said...

No chance of her advancing if it turned out she'd convicted an innocent man in her biggest, most publicized case.

Still, her conscience would not let her walk away from Daniel Logan and his quest. If the D.A. wouldn't authorize her to cooperate, she would do what she could nights, weekends and on her lunch break. To do otherwise would be wrong.

A conscience could be a real inconvenience, sometimes.

CHAPTER FIVE

DANIEL'S FAVORITE HORSE, Laramie, thundered down the polo field as Daniel focused on the ball, leaning over the horse's neck, becoming one with the surging animal.

He swung his mallet up, and with the perfect timing that happens so rarely, gave the ball a resounding thwack, launching it straight into the opposing team's goal.

A cheer went up and he brought Laramie up and swiveled him around, feeling a momentary wash of elation at seeing his teammates congratulate him.

He often invited a local polo team to play on his field, just so he could keep his hand in the sport he'd enjoyed in college and give his two ponies some exercise. He also found that the strenuous mental and physical exertion that went with playing polo helped to sweep his mind of extraneous thoughts so that he could focus more clearly on the challenges of his Project Justice work.

Today, especially, he'd needed the stress relief of a good workout. His attempts over the weekend to gather evidence he would need to free Christopher Gables had met with only limited success. Any day now, the state would set the date for Christopher's execution, and time seemed to be slipping away.

He hadn't heard from Jamie over the weekend, and it was all he could do not to call her at home or on her cell. But she had to be handled delicately. Somehow, Daniel had to juggle the urgency of his quest with his desire not to push Jamie so hard that she walked away.

The chukker was over, and it was time to change horses, give Laramie a well-deserved rest. He had just dismounted, handing Laramie off to a groom, when he spotted Jillian approaching with a determined stride and a distinct frown.

Normally she didn't let any aspects of her duties bother her on an emotional level. She was always upbeat, so a frown was out of character.

When she reached him, she handed over a cell phone to him. "Jamie McNair. You told me to put her calls through under any circumstances."

"And I meant it." He took the phone. "Yes, Jamie."

"Took you long enough."

"Jillian had to hunt me down. Sometimes I get away from all communications, just to clear my head."

"She said you were playing polo."

Jillian knew better than to give someone more information about him than they absolutely needed. "Yes, I was. Clears my head, like I said."

"Hmm. Best I can do is a little deep breathing."

"I'd be happy to teach you how to play polo," he said cheerfully, refusing to let her put him down because he had money. He'd learned long ago not to apologize for his wealth.

"No time for that, I'm afraid. I'll be over after work—around six. I hope you're free."

He smiled slightly at her high-handed tone. She was determined to prove to him he couldn't push her around because of his money and position, and she probably secretly wanted to rankle him, too. If there was one thing Jamie feared, it was that someone would view her as soft.

He suspected she had a soft side. He'd get to it eventually.

"If I'm not free, I'll rearrange my schedule. For you. We'll have dinner."

"That's not necessary."

"Yes, it is. Our brains will work much more efficiently if we—"

"Yes, yes, I've heard it before. We have to refuel our bodies."

"You don't disagree, do you?"

"I just… It seems frivolous, enjoying the sort of meals you routinely eat."

This wasn't the first time he'd run into this attitude. Some people, particularly those raised in poverty, felt guilty for treating themselves.

"I'll see if Chef Claude can rustle up some gruel and moldy bread, if you'd rather."

She actually laughed. "I'll see you at six."

"Is there a reason you're coming, or will you leave me in suspense?"

She almost whispered her next words. "Can't talk here. Have to go."

Well, that was sufficiently mysterious.

He handed the phone to a still-scowling Jillian. "What?" he asked.

"I just don't like that woman. She's high-handed and snooty."

"She's insecure, and trying to establish her authority. Cut her some slack. As you pointed out, my actions might cost her her job, and she deserves some credit for at least keeping the lines of communication open."

"But she thinks Christopher Gables is a serial killer. That's nuts…isn't it?"

"She thinks that only because she can't stomach the alternative—that she put the wrong man on death row. Eventually she'll turn around if I handle things just right."

"You like her, don't you?"

"Like her? I suppose I do." More to the point, he wanted her in his bed, but though he shared a lot with Jillian, his sexual appetite wasn't a subject he ever broached with her.

"You get all sparkly whenever you talk to her, or when her name comes up."

"Do I?"

"Maybe this is none of my business, Daniel, but if you're ready to get…romantic with someone, you can do better than her. Aside from the fact her profession is diametrically opposed to yours, she could be dangerous. People get crazy when their livelihoods, their very identities, are threatened."

Daniel took a deep breath, held it, then let it out slowly. "You're right, Jillian. It *is* none of your business."

Jamie, dangerous? To his control, yes. But she wasn't going to try to kill him.

He turned his back on Jillian to thank the guys from the polo club, but not before he saw the flash of hurt in her eyes.

Damn it, he didn't want to hurt her. She was like a kid sister to him. Their fathers had been friends, and she'd been working for his family since her teenage years.

But neither was he willing to take dating advice from her. Although he wasn't certain what she did on her days off, he didn't think she dated, either. She was as socially isolated as he was.

Maybe he should encourage Jillian to take a different job within the Logan organization. His CEO was always trying to steal her. If she worked at Logan Oil and lived away from his estate, her life would be more normal.

He made a mental note to consider the possibility further. For the first time in years, he really didn't want Jillian around, not if she was going to judge what he did—or didn't do—with Jamie McNair.

JAMIE WAS SURPRISED, and not quite prepared, when Daniel himself answered the door with Tucker at his heel.

"Come in, Jamie." He offered a brief smile, but his eyes were solemn.

"Thank you. Did your butler take the day off?"

"You know, you're going to have to get that boulder-size chip off your shoulder if we're going to work together."

"Sorry?"

"Your resentment of my wealth. Would you like me better if I gave it all away and lived in a cardboard box under a bridge?"

She stepped past him over the threshold, her heels clicking on the marble floor. "You aren't going to tell me your money is a curse, are you?"

"Far from it. I am grateful every day of my life for the circumstances I was born into. My parents gave me every opportunity, every advantage. If not for money, frankly, I'd be dead right now. Because legal skills alone would not have gotten me a pardon. It took money, too—for publicity, for lawyers, for scientific tests. My father made it his full-time job to exonerate me."

Jamie took a mental step back. When she'd fired off her crack about the butler, she hadn't expected this impassioned speech.

Did she resent his wealth? Maybe a little. As a prosecutor, she had a limited budget and limited resources. Maybe she did bristle at the fact he had unlimited supplies of both.

"The extent of your wealth overwhelms me," she said in all honesty. "I can't wrap my mind around it. But I

didn't intentionally malign your father." She squatted
down to greet Tucker and give him a little scratch behind
the ears. It was easier to look into his sweet brown eyes
than face Daniel's challenging gaze.

"No, you didn't. And maybe I overreacted. Let's go
sit down. Dinner should be ready in about an hour, is
that okay?"

"That's…that's fabulous." Whatever he served was
sure to beat the dinner she would have had on her
own—probably something frozen popped into the
microwave.

She thought he'd take her down to the basement again.
Instead, he led her down the same hallway as before,
stopping before reaching the stairs where he entered a
different room. It was a large library, probably larger
than the public library she'd checked out books from as
a child. The room was a symphony of warm wood and
leather and stone, very masculine yet somehow cozy
and inviting. An enormous stone fireplace dominated
the room, smack in the center and open on two sides.
Though it was only in the sixties outside, a low flame
burned, giving the room more intimacy than it otherwise
would have had.

Tucker headed straight to the fireplace and flopped
onto a rug in front of the raised hearth.

The walls were lined with floor-to-ceiling shelves
stuffed with all manner of books, from ancient-looking
leather-bound volumes to current bestselling novels.
At the opposite end of the room was a carved oak bar,

which appeared fully stocked with bottles and bottles of liquor lined up on mirrored shelves.

Jamie was drawn, though, to a Christmas tree. The thing had to be fifteen feet tall, a lovely, lacy cedar whose top brushed the vaulted wood-beamed ceiling.

She looked up at a string of lights, only half strung. The tree was in progress. "I'd almost forgotten that the holidays were coming."

"They're not my thing, either, but Jillian always makes a big deal about the decorating. She seems to enjoy it."

"Maybe if I had a place like this to decorate, I'd get more excited." She could almost picture a Christmas morning here, stockings hung on that enormous hearth stuffed with goodies, shiny packages under the tree, a cheerful fire—never mind that Houston Christmases were often downright balmy.

Then she imagined children squealing in delight as they discovered the presents Santa had brought, the smell of hot cocoa…

She shook her head, alarmed by the fanciful turn of her imagination. The only things she knew of squealing children on Christmas morning were what she'd seen on TV. Her mother had always worked on Christmas because she could get double time, and presents had been a foreign concept.

One time, Toys for Tots had stopped by, wanting to give Jamie a shiny wrapped package. Her mother had tartly told them she didn't accept charity.

"Jamie?"

She snapped back to reality. "Sorry. I'm curious—how do you celebrate? Do you hand out BMWs and diamond necklaces? Buy the biggest goose in town and stuff it with caviar?"

"You're doing it again."

"I am. Sorry."

"My Christmas is always low-key. I give my employees bonuses, usually a few days before the holidays so they can do something nice for themselves. Then I let them celebrate with their families."

"So you hang out here by yourself? I know your parents have passed away, but don't you have any family?"

"I like the solitude. And no, no family. Oh, some cousins in Philadelphia. I invite them to visit every year, but they haven't come since... Well, it was awkward. Small children involved, and all that."

His relatives were afraid to expose their children to him? Because they thought he was a murderer?

That thought made Jamie unbearably sad. Though she'd believed he was a killer at one time, possibly even a serial offender, she had a hard time reconciling that possibility with the man she was coming to know.

"Christmas is hardly a blip on my radar screen," she said. "No family here, either. Christmas is so overdone, anyway."

"So that's one thing we have in common," Daniel

observed. "We don't get all caught up in the holiday baloney. Probably suits you just fine, am I right?"

"Absolutely. People go crazy. They spend money they can't afford. They buy toys their kids will get tired of in a week."

"They gain weight and spend all of January feeling guilty for their excesses."

"They cut down trees that'll just end up in the land-fill." She glanced at the behemoth of a cedar.

"I turn mine into mulch and use it for the gardens."

"Well, all right, then. You're excused for the ginor-mous tree."

Daniel smiled at her, and something inside her that was hard and tight loosened just a bit. Maybe she did have a chip on her shoulder where money and privilege were concerned. She'd hated those snotty rich kids she'd gone to law school with who'd looked down on her be-cause she didn't drive the right car and wear the right labels.

Daniel did some good things with his money. Logan Oil was one of the most ecologically conscious fuel companies on the planet. The company donated mas-sive amounts of money to clean up oceans, and Daniel personally gave away lots of money to worthy causes, not to mention all he did with Project Justice.

Maybe she would never relate to his lifestyle, but that didn't mean she had to condemn him for it.

Condemn. Funny she should use that word.

"Maybe we should get down to business," she said, hoping to reel her mind in from its errant path.

"Good idea. We can work over here." He led her to a large walnut gaming table where they had plenty of room to spread out. The moment they got settled, a servant entered with a platter of hors d'oeuvres, small plates, napkins and wineglasses.

Daniel held up a hand when the servant would have poured them wine. "Not tonight, Manuel. We're working."

"Yes, sir."

Jamie's stomach was rumbling, so she availed herself of the nibbles—water chestnuts wrapped in crispy bacon, mushrooms stuffed with a wild-rice concoction, Brie and some of the tastiest crackers she'd ever sampled.

"So, Jamie, can I ask why you're here?" Daniel asked, also diving into the food. "And with a large, fully stuffed briefcase?"

Right. She'd almost forgotten the reason she'd come. "First, you have to give me your word you won't divulge what I'm about to tell you to anyone."

"If it will help free Christopher—"

"It won't."

"Okay, I give you my word."

"Good, because if it suited you, you could easily get me fired. I'm here because I want to find out what, if any, real connection exists between the Frank Sissom and Andreas Musto murders. Unfortunately, the district attorney doesn't agree that this research is necessary or appropriate. He forbade me to assist you. In fact, he ordered me to throw every possible roadblock at you."

Daniel set down the mushroom he'd been about to pop into his mouth. "Wow."

"He's my boss, and I'm supposed to support his policies. But I can't walk away. I may not agree with you about Christopher's innocence, but I want to find out what really happened. Who was the man Theresa saw in the kitchen? Where did those metal shavings come from? And who belongs to that DNA?"

"We may not want the same outcome," Daniel said. "But we both want the truth, and we can help each other."

"But I can't do this on the county's dime. My assistance is limited to evenings and weekends. And my part in this is to be kept in strictest confidence—unless and until we're prepared to take some kind of legal action, such as filing charges or making a motion to have Christopher's verdict overturned."

"Of course. Believe me, I don't want you to get fired. It's not in my best interest."

"So what about your servants? Jillian and Manuel and…the chef? Claude?"

"You can trust them. I don't allow anyone to work on the estate who hasn't been vetted six ways to Sunday. Jillian has been working for my family since before I was released from prison. Manuel's father is the head gardener here—he was raised on the estate. And

Claude—I've known Claude since high school. In fact, he was a part of my first restaurant venture right out of college."

Daniel lowered his voice. "It was a colossal failure, I'm afraid. That's when I learned that a fancy business degree and a talented chef don't add up to a successful restaurant."

"You owned a business that failed?" That surprised Jamie.

"Most restaurants fail. We made a lot of bad calls. My dad could have bailed us out, but he wanted me to learn from my mistakes. Otherwise, I'd just keep making them."

"That must have been a painful lesson. I mean, your father was a legend in business. Was it hard to live up to that?"

"Sometimes. He lived and breathed Logan Oil. I think he was disappointed when I wanted to go into the restaurant business, but he supported me. That's what I remember about him the most. He let me make my own decisions and supported me, no matter what.

"When I was arrested, he never once believed, even for a second, that I could have committed a violent crime."

Daniel's face clouded over. "The strain of those years is what killed him. My mom, too."

Jamie couldn't help but feel bad for a man who'd lost both of his parents just when he'd finally regained his freedom. "They both died within a year of your release...is that right?"

"Yeah. Dad had a massive coronary. Mom had cancer—she was already sick by the time I came home. It wasn't as happy a time as it might have been."

It struck Jamie suddenly that Daniel wasn't a happy man. He put on a good show, but deep down, he must have been very lonely. Maybe all that money *was* a curse. Especially when he didn't trust anyone, didn't let anyone close unless they were "vetted," as he put it.

"Anyway, back to work." Daniel seemed to shake off his melancholy. "I've set up a tentative appointment on Wednesday to meet with Christopher Gables. Unfortunately, it's smack in the middle of the day. If you can't make it, that's unfortunate, but I'll try to be flexible, given your new constraints."

"I could take a personal day off." She was treading in dangerous territory. If Winston found out... But she was entitled to a day off once in a blue moon, right?

THE UPCOMING VISIT to Christopher Gables became the focus of the evening. Though the work was somber in nature, Daniel actually enjoyed using his wits and collaborating with someone as bright as Jamie.

She'd brought a transcript with her of Christopher's original interrogation, which she'd already read and highlighted—she must have stayed up all night doing it. They picked apart various statements he'd made, making lists of follow-up questions and clarifications they wanted.

Sometimes, though, Daniel found his focus drifting to Jamie's hair, and how it fell across her cheek every time she looked down to read something. She would impatiently shove it behind her ear, only to have it fall again within a few minutes.

He could smell her, too.

In prison, he used to dream about the way women smelled. Whether it was baby powder, expensive perfume or flour and sugar and yeast, women smelled like nothing else in the world, and he'd sorely missed that olfactory stimulation when he'd been locked up.

Then, one day, he couldn't call it up in his imagination. Couldn't fantasize about it as he lay in his bunk. And he'd felt a panic all out of proportion. His memories, his imagination, those were all he'd had in prison to comfort him. He'd been afraid of losing his ability to think at all. Afraid of going stark-raving mad.

Was it Jamie's skin that smelled like vanilla? Her hair? Did he detect a faint scent of lipstick?

Would she taste as good as she smelled?

"So here, he says he noticed the time he got home," Jamie was saying, and Daniel snapped his attention back to her words. "Yet fifteen minutes later, he says he didn't look at the clock and didn't wear a watch. Why the discrepancy?"

"Could be a number of things. He might have turned on the TV and noticed a particular show was starting.

He might have noticed the time on his car clock right before coming in. He might have seen the time on a VCR or a coffeemaker or a microwave or even his cell phone. He might have seen how high the moon was—it was a full moon that night."

Jamie made notes. "I want to ask him."

"We'll have limited time. Are you sure it's relevant?"

"It's relevant because I can catch him lying."

They already knew Christopher was apt to make stuff up. Even if they did catch him in a lie, it wouldn't necessarily speak to his guilt or innocence. But Daniel didn't argue. He had Jamie on his side—sort of—and he didn't want to blow it.

"We have a psychologist on call—Claudia Ellison. Have you heard of her?"

"Sure. She testifies as an expert witness all the time."

"She's an expert on body language. She has watched video of Christopher Gables and feels certain he's telling the truth—about the important stuff."

"I disagree. I remember thinking, when I watched the interrogation, that he was lying."

"But you had a vested interest in his guilt."

"Which is why I want to ask him certain questions."

"With an open mind?"

"Yes, Daniel."

He sighed. "It's after seven. Claude will have dinner on the table. Let's take a break."

"Okay." She picked up a stack of papers. "I can read you this part of the transcript—"

He touched her hand and his awareness went off like a firecracker.

"We need to give our minds a break, too. If we come back fresh after dinner, we'll get more done."

"But—"

"Trust me on this. I've studied the research. Working harder doesn't necessarily mean working smarter."

She laughed. He loved the sound of her laughter, so rare and unexpected. "You sound like one of those inspirational speakers they bring in to professional development seminars."

"Busted. Once upon a time, I attended those types of seminars on a monthly basis. It was right after college, when I was intent on the success of my own business. I felt like a sponge, wanting to soak up every piece of advice anyone had to offer."

"Aren't those seminars just gimmicks? Do they really help?"

"If there's one thing I took away from that part of my education," he said as he stood, then went to pull out her chair for her, "it's that the best thing you can do for any kind of challenging mental or physical activity is take care of your body."

"That's easier to do when you have someone preparing your food."

"I'll grant you that. But I didn't always have Claude to cook for me. I lived on my own at one time."

"By yourself? No servants? No live-in administrative assistant?"

"Hard as you find it to believe that, yes. Right after college I worked for Logan Oil in the marketing department, earned a paycheck, paid rent on a condo. Provided my own meals."

"Sounds like you lived pretty normally."

"Different from now, huh?"

He took her hand—pretty, soft, with her natural fingernails painted in clear polish—and placed it firmly on his arm. His mother had taught him that when called to dinner, all ladies must be escorted to the table.

She didn't resist, but she smiled wryly. "Very courtly. Did they teach you that at finishing school?"

"Girls go to finishing school. Boys take comportment classes."

"Did you really?"

"In seventh grade I did. My mother was from Savannah, Georgia, and she insisted her only son have manners. I learned more from her, though, than any class."

Daniel led Jamie to the main dining room. Predictably, she gasped when she saw it.

"Good night! You could give a dinner here and invite the entire Texas legislature. Where do you buy a table that big? They don't sell them at the local IKEA."

Now it was his turn to laugh. "The table came from some castle in Spain."

"And the chandeliers?"

He shrugged. "Not sure. My father wanted his house to be like the homes of the well-to-do in Great Britain and Europe. He was pretentious, I'll admit it. My mother made it her job to hunt down furniture and carpets and chandeliers that would make him happy."

"I could easily believe I was in an ancient castle somewhere. But please tell me we won't be sitting at opposite ends of the table. We'll be shouting to hear each other."

She was probably just teasing, because clearly there were two places set at one end.

But Jillian hadn't used the good china, as he'd asked. He had wanted to create an oasis of comfort and beauty, so that for a few tranquil minutes they could forget about the grisly deaths they had immersed themselves in.

The ordinary stoneware and stainless cutlery were what he usually ate with outside, on the patio, where it wouldn't matter if they got broken or misplaced. And there was no tablecloth, only some brown cloth place mats.

Jillian had certainly been acting strangely. Normally she followed his wishes to a T, sometimes anticipating his wants and needs before he even spoke them. Maybe Manuel or Cora had set the table, and there'd been a miscommunication somehow.

"You're frowning."

"Oh, it's nothing." If he made a big deal about their place settings, it would only add to Jamie's opinion that he was a rich snob who didn't occupy the same earthly plane as she did.

He seated her on the side of the table, then grabbed a candelabra from the buffet and lit it, setting it nearby. Candlelight could make anything look better.

"Do you always eat dinner here?"

"Usually." He spoke briefly into the phone, alerting the kitchen staff that they were ready, then took his own chair. "When my parents were alive, they always ate a formal dinner. And they dressed for dinner, too—my mother wouldn't have dreamed of coming to the table without stockings and heels and proper jewelry."

"Daniel, I don't mean this as criticism, but your life is about as strange as it gets. You spend your days in the Batcave, analyzing TV broadcasts and going over data your people send to you, and in the evening…this. You never leave the house."

"Not never," he reminded her. "I did go downtown to see you."

"And you couldn't exit your limousine. It's not normal, even for someone with your wealth."

He didn't argue with her, because she was only telling it like she saw it. He knew he wasn't like most people. He preferred to think of it as living life on his own terms, something most people didn't have the means to do.

But Jamie thought he was weird.

The realization disturbed him. He didn't want her to see him that way. It shouldn't matter; Jamie McNair was a means to an end. He was using her position and her fine brain to help him save a man's life.

But it was impossible to remember that when he saw Jamie not as an adversary or reluctant ally, but as a beautiful, vibrant woman he would very much like to invite into his bed.

Romantic conquests had once come easily to him, and he told himself that his celibacy since prison was a choice. But the truth was, he hadn't tried to woo any woman since he'd been granted his freedom. Despite his persistent prison fantasies of willing women and nonstop bedroom acrobatics, romance and sex had fallen way down on his priority list.

His sex drive had chosen an inconvenient moment to wake up.

Not now. For the first time, he believed he stood a chance of finding the man who'd framed him for the murder of his friend. Once he did, he fully intended to dispense justice his way. And Jamie, thoroughly disillusioned, wouldn't find him at all attractive. She would try to put him behind bars.

CHAPTER SIX

JAMIE FORCED HERSELF TO RELAX. If a wealthy million-aire—some said billionaire—was determined to serve her another excellent meal, why should she argue? As he'd pointed out before, she had to eat.

But this was like something out of a movie about the Tudors or the Bourbons. At least the dishes were ordinary, though the ornate porcelain candelabra looked as if it belonged in a museum somewhere.

The door to the dining room opened, and a portly man in white entered pushing a cart filled with bowls and jars of mysterious ingredients. In his late thirties, he wore his blond hair very short. His face was flushed and jowly, and his tall chef's hat didn't quite disguise a receding hairline.

"Claude." Daniel sounded surprised. "What brings you out of the kitchen?"

Ah, so this was the mysterious Claude who concocted the brilliant food.

"I hear you have a guest," Claude said, beaming. "So I wanted to make sure things were done right." He looked over the table, then frowned. "Bah, what are those dishes?"

"A misunderstanding," Daniel said in a voice that indicated he didn't want to pursue the issue. What was that about?

"You can't eat my beef tips à la Bourgogne on such common dishes. It's heresy. I'll have them replaced with—"

"No, Claude, really, it's not necessary," Jamie interrupted. "We have a lot to get done tonight. These dishes are just fine.

"My associate, Jamie McNair," Daniel said by way of introduction. She supposed "associate" was as good a term as any.

"It is very nice to meet you, Mademoiselle Jamie. I come to make a Caesar salad fresh for you." He had a lovely French accent. "I apologize for the place setting. A beautiful lady such as yourself should only eat from the finest china."

Jamie found herself charmed. "It's all right, believe me. I usually eat my dinner out of a paper microwave box, so this is an improvement."

Claude looked pained. "Microwave. Bah."

He proceeded to make a show of sharpening a knife, then mincing several cloves of garlic so quickly his fingers blurred. Eggs, anchovies, Worcestershire sauce, mustard, olive oil, all were tossed into the dressing mix with the grace of a circus juggler, and Jamie found herself relaxing. The troubles of the day—her conflict with Winston, her growing doubts about the Christopher

Gables verdict—receded into the background as she once again allowed Daniel to delight her senses.

She applauded as Claude served her salad and added grated Parmesan and freshly sautéed crispy croutons.

The dinner was, as expected, incredible. The beef was so tender it didn't need a knife, the flavors in the rice pilaf so delicate and aromatic she wanted to linger over it. Even the string beans—normally an uninspiring vegetable—were elevated to a new level just by virtue of their freshness and simple preparation.

As Manuel cleared the table, Jillian made an appearance, dressed to the nines once again in form-fitting leather pants and a gauzy shirt, through which her black bra was clearly visible. She nodded at Jamie through slitted eyes, then turned her back and focused solely on her boss.

"I'm working on the office holiday party, and I thought it might be nice to just have it here."

"Here?"

"It's not like we don't have plenty of room for entertaining, and Claude could prepare the food. It would be cost-effective."

"I don't care about—" He stopped himself, probably not wanting to admit in front of Jamie that he didn't care about the cost. "Why don't we have it at the Windsor Hotel, like always?"

"They're booked already. And we can't change the date—we've already told everybody to save December 5."

And why was Jillian hitting him with this particular problem now, at 7:45 in the evening? Jamie wondered. It wasn't as if she could do anything about the venue tonight. But Jamie was pretty sure she knew the answer.

"Filling the house with people—it just can't be done. The security, for one thing, would be a nightmare."

"Daniel, these are your people. Your handpicked employees. You don't trust them?"

"I trust them. But their spouses, their kids—"

"We'll put them through a metal detector," Jillian said practically, and Jamie couldn't tell if she was kidding or not. "Before and after the party, so they won't be tempted to make off with the silver."

"Let me sleep on it. Jillian, really, I don't have time for something so trivial. I'm working on a case."

"Oh. I thought you were having dinner."

"A working dinner. We'll discuss this later."

Clearly she was being dismissed, and just as clearly, she didn't like it. With one last hostile glance at Jamie, Jillian left.

Dessert consisted of a thin slice of pound cake with fresh strawberries and whipped cream. Jamie longed to clean her plate, but an overfull stomach would only make her sleepy, and there was much more work to do.

She took a couple of bites, barely refraining from moaning in gustatory pleasure, then pushed the plate aside.

"No good?" Daniel asked just before forking a strawberry into his mouth.

"No room. Daniel, are you aware that your administrative assistant is in love with you?"

DANIEL STOPPED MIDCHEW, almost spewing a half-eaten strawberry across the table. "Excuse me?"

"Jillian. She's in love with you."

Daniel swallowed painfully and took a sip of water as he recovered his composure. "That's ridiculous. She's like a sister to me. I've known her since she was a kid—she worked for my mother as a summer job when she was still in high school."

"She might be a sister to you, but you're not a brother to her," Jamie said, looking faintly amused. "At first, I wondered why she disliked me so intensely."

"She doesn't dislike you, I'm sure. She doesn't even know you."

"She knows that I'm a single woman spending a great deal of time with you. How often do you bring women here to the estate?"

"It's not that rare. I bring the Logan Oil board of directors here, I conduct meetings—"

"How often do you share intimate meals with your female guests? One-on-one?"

She had him there. "Pretty much never."

"Jillian is threatened by my presence. Although we know that your interest in me is purely professional, she worries that it's something else."

"Are you sure?" If Jamie was right, he had a big problem.

"I'm positive. She already does everything a wife does—she runs your house, handles your schedule, sees to every detail of your needs. I'll bet she even buys your clothes for you."

Damn it, Jamie was right. "She doesn't do *everything* a wife does," he pointed out.

"No, but she wants to. She wants to have the Christmas party here, because then she could act as your hostess, the queen bee. She figures all she has to do is seduce you, and once you're sleeping together, all she lacks is a wedding ring."

"How long has this been going on?" he asked aloud. It was meant as a rhetorical question, but Jamie answered anyway.

"Probably since she first met you. Think about it. She's the young, impressionable girl, you're the older, sophisticated heir apparent to all this." Jamie swung her arms wide, encompassing his whole estate, he supposed. "It probably started out as a case of hero worship. While you were in prison, she waited for you."

"She went to college," he objected.

"And wrote you letters once a week, I'll bet."

Daniel winced. "Yes. One of the few people who did. Her loyalty impressed me."

"Did you write back to her?"

"Yes. What else did I have to do? Her letters cheered

me up, and it would have been rude not to acknowledge them."

"She saw it as an intimate connection, a secret you two shared, in a way. You were a romantic figure. And when you came home, she probably made it her mission to make up for what you suffered. Did she sign on as your personal assistant then?"

"Yes."

"Has she had a boyfriend in all those years?"

"Not that I know of. Jamie, you're interrogating me."

She'd been leaning across the corner of the table, almost in his face. Now she slumped back into her chair. "Sorry. It's a habit. Probably the reason I haven't had a relationship that lasted more than five minutes."

Daniel tucked that bit of information away to dissect later. Right now, he had more pressing problems. "Damn it, you're right. What am I going to do?"

"If you don't return her feelings—"

"Of course I don't. I value her and trust her as a friend, but not…" He shuddered. That would be so wrong.

"Then you should confront her and tell her. Tell her there is no chance the two of you will ever be together. You can't let her keep mooning over you."

He considered Jamie's advice. "Or," he said after a moment, "I relocate her to a different job. To Logan Oil…or, with her organizational skills, she could do wonders at Project Justice. I'll move her to her own apartment. Once she's not around me every day, she'll meet other men, develop other interests."

"That is the coward's way out."

"I never said I was brave. Oh, God, how will I function without her?"

"She's made you dependent on her, just by being so damned efficient. Cutting the ties will be good for both of you."

He really didn't like that Jamie could see things so clearly. She was an outsider. How could she know the things she knew?

Manuel entered to clear their dishes, and Daniel realized he'd forgotten completely about why Jamie was here. Time to get back to business.

"Thanks, Manuel. Say, Manuel, is Jillian in love with me?" He expected his question to evoke a laugh and a quick denial. Instead, Manuel bit his lower lip and looked away.

"It's not my place to say, sir. You always say how you don't like gossip." He grabbed some dishes and hightailed it out of the dining room.

Jamie flashed him an I-told-you-so smirk.

"I'll see about transferring her—right after the holiday party. She really does love planning events, and I don't want to ruin that for her. Now, let's get back to work."

"I'm ready."

They worked until almost midnight, mostly arguing over what to ask Christopher, and when. The way they approached this interview reflected their vastly different agendas. Once they agreed that Daniel's friendlier questions should come first, followed by Jamie's more confrontational approach, they made quick progress.

Finally, though, Jamie had to throw in the towel. "I've got an early appearance in court tomorrow," she said. "Much as I've become fascinated by these murders, I still have a job, and I owe it to the good people of Harris County to show up with some semblance of a clear mind."

"Understood. We made good progress. Tomorrow, you'll send the metal-shavings evidence to PrakTech Labs?"

"Yes." She'd been trying to figure out how to accomplish that task without Winston finding out. But he probably wouldn't. He was so busy worrying about his public image, and whether his suits were tailored correctly, that he seldom observed anything that didn't get thrust right in front of his face.

"Then I'll walk you out."

Daniel was nothing if not a gentleman. His courtliness was refreshing, if a bit archaic, in this age of supposed equality between the sexes. She found herself charmed and leery all at the same time, wondering if he was buttering her up, manipulating her for the next big thing he was going to ask of her.

"Tomorrow, I'm going to track down the mystery DNA results from both cases and send them off for comparison. I'll also submit them both to the database again. Neither could be matched years ago. It's a long shot, but the database grows every day."

"Excellent idea. And you are going to make it on Wednesday, right?"

She'd been telling herself all evening that she would have to think about it some more before committing to calling in sick on Wednesday. She'd never missed a day of work in her life, and certainly not for something so subversive.

But she never would have prepared so thoroughly for the meeting if she hadn't intended to be there.

"Yes. How will we get to Wichita Falls? It's a long drive."

"We'll fly, of course."

Of course. When money was no object, you flew wherever you wanted to go. "I'll pay for my own ticket." She didn't want her acceptance of free air travel to come back later and bite her in the butt.

"I'll send you a bill." He smiled crookedly at her, and she got the feeling she'd never see that bill.

Funny, a few days ago she never would have considered flying to a strange town with Daniel and not telling anyone. But the more time she spent with him, the harder it was to view him as a murderer. If her father had gotten to know Daniel, would he still have prosecuted the case?

Daniel held her leather jacket while she slid her arms into it, then opened the massive front door and walked her to her Subaru, which looked even smaller

and shabbier than usual in these overblown surroundings. She had to admit, though, the place was beautiful
at night—artfully lit. The fountain in the center of the
circular driveway gurgled softly.

In any other circumstances, she might have described
the surroundings as romantic. Girl, boy, alone…

No. *Keep your mind on business.*

"Jamie, thank you for coming—for everything. I
know you're taking a tremendous risk for me, and I
appreciate it."

"It's not for you."

"For Christopher, then."

"And for me. If I was wrong about Christopher…well,
it shakes my faith in the whole justice system."

"The justice system isn't perfect, because it relies on
the feelings and opinions of human beings, who are also
not perfect. People make mistakes, perfectly natural
mistakes. It's no reason to doubt yourself, or to think
you're not good at your job."

Oh, but it did. It would change everything about how
she saw her work. She still clung to the possibility that
Christopher was responsible for both murders, but she
kept that fact to herself.

"Let's touch base tomorrow." She needed to get home
and regroup. Spending so much time in this fantasyland
Daniel called home was messing with her brain.

She opened her car and climbed in, stuck her key
in the ignition, twisted and…nothing. The engine was
deader than a doornail.

"Oh, God, not now," she grumbled. Of all times and places to have car trouble. This was going to be awkward.

As she opened her door again, Daniel stopped on his way inside and turned. "Problem?"

"Dead battery." She pulled her phone out of her purse. "I'll just call my auto club. They'll come in a jiffy and give me a charge. If you can just make sure they can get through the front gate, I'll wait here for them."

"You'll do no such thing. It's late, and you need your sleep. I have a guest room waiting, and by morning your car will be ready to drive. I'll have Randall take care of it."

It must be nice to be rich! This time, though, she refrained from ribbing Daniel about his easy life.

She tried one more time. "Really, you don't have to."

"Look." He strode purposefully toward her. "I'm not going to leave you sitting out here in the cold waiting for Triple A, because I won't be able to sleep. And I value my sleep. So come inside, make both of our lives easier."

"All right. Thanks," she added reluctantly. She hated depending on him.

What if he'd tampered with her car? Now he would lure her to his den and turn her into a sex slave.

She grinned, realizing that such a fate didn't appall her as much as it should have. Daniel was definitely getting under her skin.

WHEN JAMIE AWOKE the next morning, she felt like a storybook princess. The room certainly befitted royalty, with a bed made up of pale blue satin linens and carpet she could lose her feet in.

Though she wasn't ready to face the day, she forced herself to slide out from under the feather comforter, put her feet on that fantastic carpet and head into the ridiculous bathroom.

The bathroom featured a huge shower and a whirl-pool bath, both big enough for two. Her traitorous mind couldn't help but conjure an image of herself with Daniel, naked, bodies slick with melon-scented soap as they writhed—

Damn. She had to get her mind back on business, and fast. Better make her shower water cold.

But when she turned the shower handle, the faucet didn't come on. Frowning, she tried the faucet to the whirlpool tub. Water gushed out. Oh, well, she'd take a bath instead of a shower. She used some of the vanilla-scented bath crystals sitting on a shelf above the toilet, sprinkling them into the water and creating mountains of bubbles.

The bathtub had its own flat-screen TV mounted on the wall. Perfect, she could multitask. Seeing no remote control, she pushed the power button and was about to sink into the warm, softly scented water when she remembered her washcloth. She stepped out of the water.

That was when the entire TV pulled loose from the

wall and crashed into the tub, complete with sparking, smoking wires. Jamie could actually feel the electricity in the air. The bathroom lights flickered and went out.

Her heart thudding, Jamie sank to the floor as her knees would no longer support her.

She'd just come within an inch of electrocution.

Once the immediate reaction of fear and relief wore off, anger took its place. Who would put a TV over a bathtub anyway? That was ridiculous. And if they did, why wouldn't they make sure it was securely mounted?

Gingerly, she turned off the running water, then grabbed her robe, stuffed her arms into the sleeves and cinched it closed with a tug, ready to march downstairs, find Daniel and give him a piece of her mind.

Turned out that wasn't necessary. As she plowed through the bathroom door, Daniel was rushing into her bedroom calling her name. An agitated Tucker was right behind him.

"Jamie. Oh, thank God you're okay. Security reported a huge power surge in this part of the house. I called several times and you didn't answer." To her dismay he put his arms around her and hugged her. And here she was, with only a robe on, one that was gaping at the neck.

Suddenly the anger went out of her and she got all wobbly-kneed again. "Daniel, I almost died. The TV… fell in the bath…"

"What?" He gently disengaged from the hug and led

her to the edge of the bed, so she could sit down. She tugged her robe more securely closed.

"I was running a bath. I went to turn on the TV and it fell right into the water."

Daniel marched into the bathroom and cursed colorfully. "How could this have happened? The TV shouldn't have been loose. I have one in my bathroom, too, and a jackhammer couldn't get it free from the tile."

Tucker, calmer now, sat next to Jamie and placed one big paw in her lap, as if checking to make sure she was really okay. Jamie petted him absently.

Daniel exited the bathroom, looking shaken. "Jamie, I'm so sorry. When these TVs were installed, I questioned the safety, but the company assured me they weren't a danger, even if you touched them with wet hands."

"You'd better report this to the company, then. It's a product-liability lawsuit waiting to happen, if it hasn't already."

He smiled at her. "I guess you're okay, if you're thinking like a lawyer."

"I'm okay." She picked up her cell phone, which she'd left on the nightstand. "I really need to get dressed and get going."

"Breakfast is ready whenever you are. We're eating in the breakfast room off the kitchen today."

"I don't have time. I still have to go home and change clothes." She stood and shooed him out of the room. "What about my car?"

"It's fine. A loose battery cable. Oh, and check the closet. There's probably something appropriate in your size. The dresser drawers will have, um, intimate apparel, too."

Of course they would.

As soon as he left the bedroom, the lights came back on. No way was Jamie getting near that bathtub again. She settled for a quick scrub-down with a wet washcloth, then opened the closet and found several clothing selections, including a delicious gray wool suit in a size 8, designer label, that still had the tags. Everything he'd promised was there—including new undies still in the package.

Amazing. She could skip a trip home and eat breakfast instead. The fact that she wanted to share breakfast with Daniel, almost more than anything right now, surprised her.

THAT WAS THE SECOND TIME Daniel had spontaneously hugged Jamie McNair. He'd never been a hugger.

As he headed down the stairs, Tucker trotting ahead of him, Daniel pondered the meaning of his recent behavior. The first time he'd hugged her, he'd been grateful. This time, he'd been overwhelmed with relief that Jamie was okay.

Having spent so much time with her lately, both physically and in his mind, he felt strangely close to her. But close enough for his arguably inappropriate physical contact?

Jillian met him in the sunny breakfast room, a large, glass-walled enclosure filled with plants. The floor had been crafted from antique Mexican tiles. The room always felt good to him, warm and cheerful.

Jillian looked a crisp, wintry contrast in ice-blue wool and cashmere.

"Daniel, what's going on? A power surge?"

"A TV in the blue guest room fell in the bath. Almost fried Jamie McNair to a crisp. Jillian, I want you to call the company that installed those TVs—"

"Wait. Jamie McNair is…here?" Her face turned icy, like her outfit.

"She had car trouble last night. Seemed easier to just let her stay over."

"Car trouble. And then she almost died from a TV in the bath? And you don't see through her act?"

"Jillian," he said sternly.

"Daniel." She lowered her voice, too. "I know you think this woman is the cat's pajamas, but have you gone crazy? She probably sabotaged her own car, then rigged the TV to fall in the water. Think about it. Those TVs don't just fall off the walls."

"This one did. And you're wrong to insinuate that Jamie is to blame." Although, now that he thought about it, it was odd that he hadn't immediately suspected some nefarious plot on Jamie's part.

She could have easily disconnected a battery cable on her car. But if she did, it would be on his security video. What if she'd instigated some plan to blame him for her near-death, to distract him enough that he would be forced to give up the Christopher Gables case?

"You see it now, don't you?" Jillian said, a note of triumph in her voice.

He refused to give Jillian the point. "Just make the call. I'll deal with Jamie. And let Tucker outside, please."

As Jillian stalked out of the room, dragging a reluctant Tucker by the collar, he picked up the phone and pushed the button that would instantly connect him to his on-site security office. "Doug?"

"Brandon, sir."

"Oh, right. I need you to review some video. I had a guest arrive last night in a blue Subaru. Check the video from the driveway cam and see if she opened the hood of her car when she got out, or if she came straight to the front door. Then check to see if anyone tampered with the car while she was inside," he added as an afterthought.

"Yes, sir."

"Let me know ASAP."

There. He'd done his due diligence, and he would be pleased to prove Jillian wrong.

Why wasn't he more suspicious of Jamie? But the thought that she might have a malicious agenda hadn't crossed his mind until...well, frankly, until Jillian brought up the possibility.

Then, a terrible thought occurred to him. What if *Jillian* was somehow responsible? Jamie claimed his personal assistant was in love with him. What if she was jealous of Jamie and wanted to get rid of her somehow?

No. In the first place, he couldn't see her putting her hands into a car engine, or doing a complex sabotage of a TV. He knew Jillian. She could be stubborn, and she liked things a certain way, but she wasn't devious, and no way was she homicidal.

This was just a series of unfortunate accidents, nothing more.

CHAPTER SEVEN

A FEW MINUTES LATER, Jamie joined Daniel in the breakfast room. She'd obviously found appropriate clothing in her closet, because she definitely hadn't been wearing the gray suit and hot-pink blouse yesterday. The suit's snug, short skirt hugged her bottom, and Daniel had to force himself not to stare.

"You look nice," he said.

"I ought to. A prosecutor's salary couldn't begin to pay for this suit. But I'm grateful for it. I'll have everything cleaned and returned to you as soon as possible."

He waved away her concerns. "Keep it. It looks good on you."

"I'm not allowed to accept gifts from constituents. I'll have a hard enough time explaining why I'm wearing such an expensive suit."

It definitely was a nice suit. He recognized the quality, but would her coworkers? He didn't think so.

Cora brought in a cart with their breakfast choices—eggs, toast, bacon and sausage, fresh fruit and yogurt, and his favorite Kona coffee.

Jamie eyed the choices with a troubled expression. "I don't usually eat breakfast."

"Now that is a terrible mistake."

"I've always heard you shouldn't skip it, but then I get to running late..." She chose fruit, yogurt and one slice of whole-wheat toast, dry.

He put an almost identical choice on his plate. "Have you made a decision about tomorrow?"

"Yes. After putting in all this preparation, I want to go to Wichita Falls. I'll take a personal day."

"Good." A wave of pleasure washed over him at the knowledge he would likely spend the whole day with Jamie. But then he remembered exactly where they were going, and his pleasure diminished. When he'd walked out of the Conklin Unit six years ago, he never in a million years imagined he would ever willingly return, even as a visitor.

"I'll pick you up at seven tomorrow morning."

His phone rang, and Jamie nodded. "Go ahead."

"Brandon?"

"Yes, sir. The subject came straight to the front door, and no one got near the car."

Daniel's spirits lifted, as if a lead weight had been lifted from his stomach. "Thank God."

"Pardon?"

"Thank you, Brandon."

THE NEXT MORNING, as Jamie rifled through her closet, looking for something prison chic, her gaze fell upon the gray suit and pink blouse, which she'd neatly folded last night in anticipation of taking them to the cleaner's.

That suit had caused her no end to problems. She'd known it was a high-quality piece of clothing, but she didn't pay attention to which designers were hot or how much their stuff cost. She usually bought her clothes at outlets or department stores on sale. She bought whatever looked professional, fit well, felt comfortable and didn't break her bank account.

Some of her associates, however, took a keen interest in clothing. She hadn't been at the office ten minutes before someone asked her where she'd gotten the Tonio Cucci suit and how she'd been able to afford it.

She hadn't dared mention Daniel. Put on the spot, she'd finally choked out something about borrowing it from a friend. Then, first chance she got, she performed a Google search on Tonio Cucci and discovered her suit retailed for over a thousand dollars.

Daniel bought thousand-dollar ladies' suits to hang randomly in his guest-room closets, on the off chance some female guest would need such a thing?

The depth of his wealth once again boggled her mind. She might go as far as putting a new toothbrush in her guest room, not that she often had sleepover guests. But a selection of designer outfits in various sizes for every occasion…no.

That was crazy.

Last night, she'd started to feel something kind of warm and squiggly inside of her whenever Daniel innocently touched her arm or her shoulder, or when he became passionate about a point he was trying to make, and even when he alluded to the trial that convicted him.

She'd stopped thinking of him as a convicted murderer who'd gotten out on a technicality, and started thinking of him as a man, one with whom she actually had things in common. Someone she could talk to and never run out of conversation. Someone who challenged her on every level.

Yes, all right, she might have even spun a little romantic fantasy about him. That they could somehow become…involved. That once they'd finished with this Christopher Gables thing, they could watch a movie together or…or…

Play polo?

C'mon, Jamie. He was so far out of her league, operating in a completely different universe than she did, and the suit proved it. Once they were done with Chris Gables, they would have nothing else in common.

And, more to the point, once they were done, one of them was likely to be very disappointed in the outcome. If Project Justice freed Gables, she would feel that the system had failed. And if she succeeded in tying Christopher to the Andreas Musto murder, Daniel wasn't just going to be disappointed, he was going to feel a whole range of emotions.

It was almost seven. Jamie quickly made a decision, grabbing a pair of loose black pants with a rather boxy jacket, a high-necked blouse and low heels. Early in her career, she'd once made the mistake of wearing a skirt to a prison. When she'd had to walk past the exercise yard she'd heard so many catcalls, wolf whistles and disgusting suggestions she'd wanted to run away and take a bath.

She caught herself wondering what Daniel would think of her choice, then censored herself. Did she want to be like one of those pathetic women who sent Daniel love letters and stood outside the gate to his home, hoping for a glimpse of him?

She grabbed her briefcase and tape recorder, then at the last minute, a coat, because Wichita Falls was farther north and it might actually be cold there in November.

As she stepped out onto the porch of her town house, a gorgeous black Bentley—not the limo—pulled up in front. How many luxury cars did Daniel own?

As luck would have it, her neighbor Frances was just coming out to get her paper. She stopped and gawked at the Bentley.

Jamie groaned inwardly. Why couldn't he have sent a normal car? Why did everything with Daniel have to be a grand gesture?

"Is that gorgeous vehicle for you?" Frances asked in awe.

"Um, yeah." How did she explain this? "I'm doing some pro bono work for a charitable foundation. The car belongs to the man who runs it." That was all true.

"I'm gonna start volunteering more," Frances said wistfully.

Jamie didn't have time to worry about what Frances thought. The driver, a muscular man in a uniform, had just gotten out and was coming around to open her car door.

"Good morning, Ms. McNair," the man said with a friendly smile. "I'm Randall, your driver."

"I'd be more comfortable riding in the front." She wasn't the type of woman who rode in the backseat like some pampered princess.

"If that's your preference," Randall said, and opened the door for her.

"I can open my own doors, you know."

"Yes, you look very strong to me," Randall said with a perfectly straight face. "But opening your door is my job. You don't want to get me fired, do you?"

She rolled her eyes and got in.

Randall was fast on his feet, and moments later he was behind the wheel and putting the big vehicle in motion, whistling a little tune.

"How long have you worked for Daniel?" she asked.

"Oh, a long time. Since his college days."

"Is he nice to work for?"

"The best, ma'am. His daddy, too. The Logans are good people. Most of the senior staff has been around since before the, um, incident."

"Since before Daniel's arrest."

"Yes. Even though I was no longer needed to drive Daniel around or protect him, Mr. Logan, Sr., kept me on, found other duties for me. He was always sure Daniel was coming home. Everybody felt that way. We all knew he couldn't have done what they said, that it was just a terrible mistake."

"Eventually, you were proven right." About him coming home, at least.

"Yes, ma'am."

"Are we going to Intercontinental or Hobby?" Jamie asked. She hadn't thought to find out which airport they were using.

"Neither. Mr. Logan keeps his plane at a private airport just north of town."

"His… He has a plane?"

"It belongs to Logan Oil, but Daniel can use it anytime he needs."

"Does he, um, fly it himself?"

"He has a pilot's license, and he used to fly the Piper Cub quite a bit. But he doesn't fly jets."

Jets. They were flying a private jet to Wichita Falls.

She couldn't help herself. She felt a little thrill wiggle up her spine at the idea that she, Jamie McNair, the poor girl in the thrift-store clothes who never had enough money to go to the movies with her friends, was in a Bentley, on her way to a private airport, so that she could ride in a private jet with an oil billionaire.

She couldn't even tell anyone!

Once she had resolved Christopher's guilt or innocence, she might be forced to go public with her Project Justice work. Until then, she didn't want anyone to know, not if she wanted to keep earning a paycheck.

What she was doing wasn't unethical. She'd taken a personal day, and she hadn't specified what she would be doing. But Chubb would flip his wig if he found out she had not severed herself from Daniel and his problematic quest for justice.

The small airport was just outside town, and Randall drove the limo right up to the runway, where a sleek, gleaming jet with the Logan Oil logo on the side sat waiting.

"Let me get the door," Randall said, and for some reason, she let him. She could play the princess for a short while. No one was here but Daniel's own people, and she gathered they were discreet or he wouldn't allow them near.

The hatch was already open, providing steps into the cabin. Randall walked her the few feet toward the stairs, then followed her as she ascended, ducked her head and entered the aircraft.

Good night.

The cabin smelled of new carpeting and leather, and it looked less like an aircraft and more like the living room of a luxury home. Sofas and chairs upholstered in buttery suede were arranged here and there around tables of various sizes that were antique mahogany, or at least disguised to look that way. The furniture, of course, was bolted to the floor—the only concession to aircraft decor. Expensive-looking curtains hung over the windows.

Finally, Jamie's gaze zeroed in on Daniel, who sat in the center of it all like king of all he surveyed.

He stood to greet her. "Nice day for flying."

Her mouth automatically went dry. She'd thought her borrowed suit was nice, but the one he was wearing... it was just wool and thread and buttons, but somehow it made him look like the billionaire he was.

"So tell me again why we couldn't just take a commercial flight?"

"Because I don't fly common carriers," he said easily, though something in his eyes told her he was uncomfortable with her question. "It's a security issue. Because of my position with Logan Oil, my life is insured for an unusually large sum, and my insurance company has certain mandates about how I travel."

"But statistically a private plane is less safe than a commercial jet," she pointed out.

"Yes, but my plane doesn't allow any nutcases on board. There are lots of people who don't like me. Disgruntled former employees, antioil fanatics and a host of people who don't like the work of Project Justice. Trust me, a private plane is safer—not to mention more comfortable. Have a seat."

"Anywhere?"

"Anywhere you like. No assigned seating on Logan Air."

She chose a love-seat-size sofa at random, still amazed that this living room would soon be airborne.

"Good morning, Randall," Daniel greeted his chauffeur.

"Good morning, sir."

"Randall's coming with us?" Jamie asked.

"In addition to being a fantastic chauffeur, Randall is the best bodyguard in the world. He's former Secret Service on the presidential detail. I figure if the president trusted him, that's good enough for me."

Jamie eyed Randall curiously from the corner of her eye. He looked ordinary enough, harmless even, with his cherubic face and eyes full of humor.

But she knew appearances could be deceiving. She had prosecuted murderers who looked like innocent kids who shouldn't even be shaving yet, much less killing someone.

"I'm sure you'll be interested to hear that I've solved the mystery of the falling TV. The company that originally installed it rushed out when I told them of the accident. Apparently, the cement they used hadn't cured properly, and they took complete responsibility. So rare these days. They'll be sending you a letter of apology and offering you a free TV."

"Really. You're not going to sue them?"

"Are you?" he countered.

She shook her head. "Despite my profession, I'm not the litigious kind. I spend enough hours in the courtroom."

"I hope to never see the inside of another courtroom as long as I live."

The jet was under way quickly, and Cora—the nice woman who had served them breakfast yesterday—brought out coffee and a tray of fresh Danishes.

Since Jamie had skipped breakfast, she availed herself of the refreshments, which she knew would be excellent. But Daniel, for the first time since she'd met him, didn't seem interested in eating.

"Have you had breakfast already?" she asked.

"What? Oh. Um, no, but I can't eat right now."

"You wouldn't let me get away with that. You'd give me a speech about how we need to fuel our bodies for the tough work ahead."

"Yeah, well, that only applies if you don't have a thousand hyperactive gremlins in your stomach."

She immediately felt contrite for ribbing him. "Oh, Daniel, I'm sorry, I didn't mean to tease a man when he's not feeling well. Are you a nervous flier?" No, that couldn't be it. He had a pilot's license.

"Today I'm a nervous flier. Do you know this is the first time I've been out of Houston in three years?"

"Really? I would assume with this jet at your disposal, along with almost unlimited disposable income, you'd be jetting all over the place. I would."

"You like to travel?"

"I don't know. I've never done much of it. But if I had your resources…yes, I think I'd travel the world."

"I've done my share of that," Daniel said. The distraction of having a conversation seemed to relax him slightly. "But it gets old."

"Traveling? Strange hotels, living out of a suitcase?"

"I don't mind that so much. But it's the spending money that gets old. I've always known that I would work, like my father, doing something I enjoyed, doing something that mattered to people."

"Is that why you opened a restaurant?"

"That was a start. I thought providing high-quality food at a moderate price so everyone could afford it was a noble idea. I had a lot of ideas about things I wanted to accomplish, changes I wanted to make in the world with my money."

"You are making a difference in the world," she pointed out. "I'm a prosecutor and I'm supposed to hate you, but realistically, I know you do sometimes correct mistakes that people in my profession make."

"So you don't hate me?"

"Of course not. I'm still not convinced I'm wrong about Christopher Gables, but I'm keeping an open mind."

"That's a lot more than most D.A.s will do. You're okay, Jamie McNair."

She felt ridiculously pleased by his approval. Automatically, she wondered whether he was buttering her up for some kind of manipulation. But then she decided to just take the compliment at face value.

"You're not bad yourself, Daniel Logan."

He flashed her a genuine, warm smile, and she found herself smiling back, almost wanting to giggle with giddiness. She had found a friend in the most unlikely place, and her fantasies about becoming more than friends returned to life.

When they were close to their destination, they did a quick review of how they would approach Christopher, but Jamie could tell Daniel's heart wasn't in it, and soon they lapsed into silence. The closer they got to Wichita Falls, the more tense Daniel became—drumming his fingers on the table, getting up and walking around in circles like a cooped-up cat that longed to be free.

She wasn't used to seeing him like this. He was normally so composed, so in control.

"Is something wrong?"

"No," he said brusquely.

Well, okay, then.

They finally touched down at some other small airport. Basically it was an airstrip in the middle of a soybean field. As soon as the jet came to a stop, a limousine cruised up to within a few feet.

Randall appeared to open the hatch and lower the stairs. He was quite the multitalented man. He descended the steps first, apparently checking things out, because it was only when he called up to them that it was safe to deplane that Daniel felt ready to descend.

"Ladies first."

She smiled at his gallantry. When was the last time anyone had referred to her as a lady? Certainly no one she faced in a courtroom, where she enjoyed a good verbal brawl with the best of 'em.

As she reached the bottom of the steps, Daniel himself offered his hand to steady her for the last, bigger step to the tarmac. The electricity that shot through her with the physical contact was more likely to make her fall than anything. But somehow she managed to alight without any ungainly sprawls onto the blacktop.

It felt good, his protectiveness. No one ever worried about her or treated her like a fragile flower. "Thanks," she said as he continued to hold her hand.

Finally he let it go.

Randall ushered them into a rented limo. Jamie scooted to the far side, clutching her briefcase in front of her like a shield against the sudden, potent attraction for this unlikely man. If she could flush it out of her system somehow, she would. Getting ambushed by it every time she turned around was wearing her down.

"Here goes nothing," she murmured as the car got under way.

Daniel still didn't appear his usual, exuberant self. He stared out the tinted window, looking pale and a little green, and she was starting to get worried about him.

"Sure you're okay?" she asked again.

"I'm fine." His tone indicated he was anything but.

It took almost no time at all for the limo to reach the James T. Conklin Unit. It was in the middle of empty, treeless agricultural lands, surrounded by soybean and sorghum fields. A long driveway led up to a series of nondescript, one-story buildings.

Conklin was one of the newer Texas correctional facilities, a maximum-security unit that had been housing death-row inmates for about fifteen years. The prison's security and reputation were very good, but that didn't make Jamie any more eager to enter the gate.

Randall pulled their car up to a guardhouse, where he exchanged a hushed conversation with a uniformed woman who apparently had been prepared for their arrival. Soon they were ushered into a visitor's lot. A warden was waiting for them, ready to personally escort them into the cell block where Christopher resided.

Visits like this to prisoners whose appeals had run out were rare enough that the prison personnel took special notice, she supposed.

Randall opened her door first, so she was first to greet the warden.

"Good morning." She read the name tag identifying him as Bill Palusky and extended her hand. "I'm Jamie McNair."

"The Houston prosecutor."

"Yes, but today I'm visiting in an unofficial capacity. Thank you for seeing us."

"It's not every day someone like Daniel Logan visits our facility," the jovial Palusky replied, shaking her hand vigorously. But his eyes looked past her, into the limo, where Randall patiently held Daniel's door.

Finally Daniel emerged with a pasted-on, polite

smile, and he shook the warden's hand, too, with a barely audible greeting.

"We'll go this way." Palusky indicated a concrete sidewalk. A row of dead pansies lined the walkway, as if someone had made a futile effort to cheer the place up.

Nothing could cheer this place up.

When she successfully prosecuted a case and sent a man or woman to prison, she usually felt good about getting a dangerous person off the streets. But she tried not to think too hard about exactly where they went, or what happened to them once they arrived.

As they made their way toward the building, Palusky chatted happily about the prison band he'd started up. His whole demeanor seemed such a stark contrast to the place he worked. But she supposed you had to have rose-colored glasses to enjoy working here.

She noticed that Daniel and Randall lagged behind her and Palusky, engaged in a hushed conversation. The warden stopped, looking back uneasily.

"I'm sorry, Mr. Logan, but your group needs to stay together."

Daniel skidded to a stop, and when he looked up, Jamie realized he truly was ill. Every bit of color had drained from his face.

"Daniel!" She strode back to his side in two seconds. "What's wrong?"

"Give me a minute…" He closed his eyes, and his

Adam's apple bobbed up and down as he swallowed several times.

Jamie cast a questioning look at Randall, but the chauffeur's attention was firmly on his employer. "You okay, Daniel?"

Daniel shook his head slightly and opened his eyes. "I'm sorry, Jamie."

CHAPTER EIGHT

GOD, JAMIE THOUGHT, she'd been so stupid. This was the same prison Daniel had been sent to. Of course he would feel sick at the thought of returning to the place where he'd spent six no-doubt miserable years of his life, believing he was going to die.

"It's…it's the smell." Daniel shook his head again, as if trying to rid himself of something.

"You don't have to explain," she said, all businesslike. "We'll reschedule—"

"No, Jamie. I'm not going to make Christopher wait because I'm feeling…squeamish. Who knows how much time he has left. I can do this."

Randall, who'd surreptitiously grabbed Daniel's wrist to check his pulse, looked grave. "Not a good idea, boss. Your heart is beating so fast you're about to stroke out."

"I'll conduct the interview by myself," Jamie said decisively. "We went over our questions so many times, I know the information you're seeking. I'll be fine. I've done lots of prison interviews."

Never mind that they'd spent hours talking about the dynamic of having both of them there, playing off each other. She wouldn't be responsible for Daniel having a stroke.

"Go," she said to Randall. "I've got this covered."

Daniel cursed softly, but he didn't fight Randall when the other man urged him to retreat.

"Just a minute, you can't—" Palusky, no longer quite as jovial, pulled a radio from his pocket and spoke briefly into it. Moments later a guard appeared. "See Mr. Logan to his car," Palusky instructed, pointing toward the rapidly receding figures of Daniel and Randall. "Make sure he's okay."

Palusky looked dubiously at Jamie. "That didn't go as planned."

"It's not what Daniel planned, either, I assure you," she said. "He hasn't been feeling well all day. But I'd still like to see Mr. Gables."

The warden nodded. "I'll take you."

She was escorted to a rather strange room. It was about the size of a large walk-in closet with a partition running right down the center. On her side, two surprisingly attractive upholstered chairs and an oak table. She could see the other half of the room through a large, thick glass window. Its furnishings were much more basic, industrial-looking and probably indestructible. A metal grate just under the window allowed visitors and inmates to hear each other.

She waited about five minutes; finally a noise on the other side alerted her to Christopher's presence. She stood, ready with her polite greeting, but she didn't get the chance to use it.

"What the hell are you doing here?"

"Good morning, Mr. Gables. I'm Jamie McNair—"

"I know who you are!"

"I'm not here as a prosecutor," she said quickly. "I'm consulting with Project Justice on your—"

"Oh, that's just rich! *You're* working on my case, the bitch that screwed me over and sent me to this hellhole?"

Preoccupied as she'd been with worries about Daniel, Jamie hadn't thought through how Christopher Gables would react to seeing her, and her alone, waiting on the other side of the glass partition.

"Please, Mr. Gables, if you'll hear me out—"

"Where's Daniel Logan? I don't want to talk to you. He's supposed to be here."

Gables looked awful. During the trial, he'd had glistening blond hair and a clean-shaven, childish face. Now his hair was buzzed short, his cheeks lean, his body thin, and he sported a scraggly goatee.

"Unfortunately Mr. Logan has been detained," Jamie said. "Can we just start over here?"

"Like hell. I'm not talking to you. You're the devil. The devil's concubine." He hit the glass with his fist, and Jamie jumped back, her heart pumping wildly. "If you're consorting with my last hope, then I best get my affairs in order 'cause I'm about to meet my maker."

"Listen to me, Christopher. Things have changed. We

have new evidence, and I'm no longer convinced of your guilt." At least not one hundred percent. "Think what it could mean, having your former prosecutor pulling for your innocence." Not that she was there yet. Looking at the man now, it was quite easy to believe he could kill. His eyes had a slightly crazed look, and he'd lost a tooth.

"Forget it. I'm not talking to you, with your tricky questions and the way you twist words and make people believe stuff that you just made up out of thin air. You don't fool me. You're here to make sure I get the needle, aren't you?"

He turned his back on her and pushed a buzzer, and moments later a guard opened the door. Christopher, suddenly meek, offered up his wrists to be cuffed.

"Christopher, please wait. Please talk to me."

He ignored her. The guard looked at her, shrugged and escorted Christopher out of the room.

Suddenly Jamie wanted out of this place. It reeked of hopelessness. And she was behind a locked door. What if they didn't let her out?

For one crazy moment, she understood Daniel's fear. This moment, she was completely under the prison guards' power. No one but Daniel and his staff even knew she was here. What if she just disappeared, never came out?

She pushed the buzzer. Pushed it multiple times as an irrational panic threatened to overcome her.

Then the door opened, and Palusky was waiting for her. "What happened?"

She took a deep breath to calm herself. "He won't talk to me. Not without Daniel."

"I'm sorry you came all this way for nothing. Perhaps you can reschedule when Mr. Logan is, um, feeling better."

"Sure." But Jamie didn't see that happening. Daniel would have to turn this case over to one of his people, someone who could meet Gables face-to-face.

Damn, she needed answers from Gables. But he didn't have to talk to anyone if he didn't want to. They had no way to pressure him, no way to entice him since he'd obviously lost hope that anyone could save him.

Palusky escorted her to the parking lot, but the limousine was nowhere to be seen. Hmm. Daniel wouldn't leave her stranded here. She realized her cell phone was turned off—she hadn't wanted any interruptions during the interview. When she switched it on, she had a text from Daniel, short and sweet:

limo returning 4U shortly

"The car is on its way," she told Palusky. "You don't have to wait here with me."

Palusky shook his head. "Forgive me for saying so, but this entire episode has been odd. I think I'd like to wait with you."

He probably wanted to personally see her off the

property and make sure they weren't trying to smuggle weapons or aid in an escape. Stranger things had happened, so she couldn't blame him.

An awkward fifteen minutes later, the limo finally reappeared. She was relieved to see Randall hop out from behind the wheel.

"I'm sorry to have kept you waiting, Ms. McNair. Are you ready to go?" He opened the back door for her.

She nodded and climbed into the car's luxurious interior. She didn't expect to see Daniel, so she wasn't surprised to find herself alone.

As soon as Randall climbed behind the wheel, Jamie lowered the glass partition. "Is Daniel okay?"

"He's waiting for you at the airport."

"You didn't answer my question."

"'Okay' is a term that calls for speculation."

So, in other words, no, he wasn't okay. "I'm sorry I fell into lawyer mode there for a minute."

"It's all right. Sometimes Daniel's behavior can try the most patient of souls."

She wouldn't call it trying. Scary, more like it.

"Did the interview go okay?" Randall asked. "It didn't last very long."

"'Okay' is a term that calls for speculation." Although she trusted Randall because Daniel did, she didn't think it appropriate to report to anyone but Daniel himself about this latest catastrophe.

As soon as the car pulled up close to the plane, she didn't wait for Randall to open her door. She got out, hooked her briefcase over her shoulder and climbed the stairs toward the open hatch.

Daniel was pacing the cabin as she stepped inside. When he caught sight of her he stopped, looked at his watch, then looked back at her.

"What the hell happened? You're not supposed to be back yet."

As if this was her fault? She got in his face, surprised at the anger that welled up inside her. "What happened, Daniel, is that Christopher Gables refused to talk to me. He was expecting you. He got me—the woman who put him behind bars."

"Did you explain—"

"I tried. He was not in any mood to listen." She wrestled with the briefcase until she was free of it and tossed it onto one of the recliners.

"So we have nothing?"

"We have nothing." She slumped onto the sofa, dejected. "I've risked my job, my whole career, to get cursed at and threatened by a guy who really doesn't seem to want anybody's help."

Daniel shook his head. "I was afraid of that."

She looked at him suspiciously. "What do you mean?"

"From what the warden told me, Christopher wasn't too keen about this meeting. Said he'd been screwed over by the system so many times, had his hopes raised only to have them dashed, that he didn't believe anyone could help him."

"And you didn't see fit to warn me?"

Daniel rubbed his temples as if he had a headache. "I thought I'd be able to relate to him. I thought…"

"You thought he'd be so impressed with the big-shot billionaire oilman that you could weasel past his hostility."

"Yeah, something like that." He looked at her squarely. "I've hosed this up, haven't I?"

"I'd wager we won't get another chance to talk to Christopher Gables. Even that smiley-faced warden was unhappy with us by the time I left."

"It takes a lot of time and effort to move around a prisoner who's in isolation."

"Isolation?"

"Death-row inmates are always isolated from the other prisoners. Surely you knew that."

"I guess I don't think about it much."

"I do."

Damn. She'd been so focused on how today's events had inconvenienced and frustrated her that she'd forgotten how Daniel must feel. She wasn't exactly a ten on the warm-fuzzy scale, but today she'd reached a new level of heartlessness.

Randall chose that moment to come through the hatch and close it behind him. "Back home?"

Daniel nodded. "Nothing else we can do here, that's for sure."

Perhaps sensing his boss's black mood, Randall disappeared into the cockpit, where the company might be better.

Daniel walked over to a fold-out, self-service bar and selected a highball glass. "Drink? I have some thirty-year-old single-malt McClelland's on board."

"The kind that costs, like, $10,000 a bottle?"

He shrugged. "I just know it tastes good."

Jamie glanced at her watch. It wasn't even noon. What the hell. She didn't like Scotch, but she'd never tried the best. "Might as well drown our sorrows."

Daniel made a production out of putting ice in the glasses with a pair of fancy silver tongs, then measuring out exactly one dram and adding water.

He'd taken off his jacket and tie, opened his shirt and rolled up his sleeves, though the cabin felt quite cool to Jamie. As she watched him work, some of her irritation washed away. He was such a gorgeous man. Observing him was like looking at a magnificent painting in a museum. Except this painting walked and talked—and hurt.

She could see the pain in his every gesture now. Maybe it was always there, and she'd missed it before. Maybe he was only now dropping his guard enough to show her how he felt.

All she knew for sure was that she shouldn't have bitten his head off like that.

He took an experimental sip of his drink, nodded with satisfaction and brought the other drink to her.

"Mr. Logan, we're cleared for takeoff," the pilot's

voice said from the overhead speaker. A seat-belt sign simultaneously lit up.

Daniel sat next to her, rather than across the way. She set her drink in the armrest cup holder and fastened her seat belt. Once they were both strapped in, Daniel held his glass aloft. She grabbed hers and joined him in a toast.

"I can't even think of anything to make a toast to," he said glumly. "I might have just cost a man his life."

Jamie drew back her glass before it came into contact with his. "No. It's not your fault"

"Whose fault do you suggest it is?"

"In the first place, this was just one step in the process. We've had a setback, but it's not insurmountable. I'm not sure Gables would have told us anything useful, anyway."

"Part of my reason for wanting you here was so you could gauge his sincerity. Now you think even less of him than you did before."

"I'm not abandoning the case, Daniel."

"Really?" He seemed genuinely surprised. "I wouldn't blame you if you did."

"Nothing that happened here erased the questions I have about these two crimes."

"Then maybe I have something to drink to after all." He took another sip of his Scotch, and she felt obligated to taste the expensive liquor herself, given that her glass probably held at least $500 worth of the stuff.

Oh, God. It was horrible. She only barely managed

not to spit her mouthful out onto the plush carpet. It burned all the way down her throat, and she wasn't able to stifle a cough.

"Not good?"

"I've heard it's an acquired taste, but I don't think I'm sufficiently motivated to cultivate a Scotch-friendly palate." She set the glass aside.

"Don't worry, I'll drink it."

"Daniel…what happened back at the prison?"

"Aside from me turning into a gibbering idiot and nearly tossing my cookies in a parking lot? Nothing much."

"I *know* what happened. I mean, I was there, I saw. Was it a flashback? Do you have post-traumatic stress disorder?"

"Aren't you the curious one all of a sudden."

"I'm not asking out of morbid curiosity. I need to know. Remember that first day we met? You said you made it a priority to learn as much as possible about the people you worked with. Well, that goes for me, too. If we're going to continue to work together, I need to know what's going on. I don't want to put you in another situation—"

"Jamie. We won't be working together. It should be obvious to you that I'm not capable of handling a case of this caliber on my own. I'll reassign it to Ford or Raleigh. I should have done it in the first place. But I thought…"

"You thought because of all you and Gables had in common, you'd be the most effective investigator."

"Exactly. But clearly I was wrong. I'm fine in a research or advisory capacity—which I can do from the safety of my home. But I'm not fit to... I'm broken, Jamie."

She longed to tell him that no, there was nothing wrong with him. Every person you passed in the street had problems, phobias, dark pasts, bad dreams, whatever. But she couldn't deny that Daniel's problems were a little darker than average.

Jamie had no brave words of wisdom, no advice, no comforting sentiments. The one thing she could possibly offer was compassion, an emotion she wasn't exactly famous for.

But she did feel something for Daniel. She'd seen the clever, funny persona he showed to the world, she'd seen the intense, intelligent side of him, the part of him that cared deeply. And now she'd seen his pain.

Something inside of her awakened and responded to all of him. She laid a hand on his bare arm just as the jet began its acceleration down the runway. His muscles tensed beneath her hand, as if he didn't want her comfort or her lame attempt at understanding him.

But he didn't pull away.

"I know I can't come close to imagining how bad it was for you. I wish I could help."

"The best therapists money could buy all took a crack

at me." His voice held a touch of bitter humor. "What could you do that they couldn't?"

I could be with you. I could love you.

The thought came out of left field. Love him?

Oh, no. Her mother didn't teach her much worth remembering, but one lesson Jamie had learned well was that you never fell in love with a man who needed fixing. You never fell in love with "a project." You never fell in love with a man's potential or assumed that your love could heal them.

Every man her mother was with—and there were a lot—needed fixing. They were either alcoholics or drug users, unemployed, uneducated or undermotivated, had physical and mental disabilities or were just plain lazy or crazy.

She was not falling into that trap. Much as she was drawn to Daniel, as crazy hot as their chemistry appeared to be, she was most certainly not going down that road.

Thank God she hadn't said anything stupid out loud.

There was one thing she could do for him, and she was willing. "You're right, I can't undo the damage of six years on death row. But that doesn't mean I give up on you. I don't want you to turn over this case to an associate. I don't want to start over with someone new. We can move forward, with or without Gables's cooperation."

"You really want that?"

"I wouldn't say it just to make you feel better. I'm not that nice."

He smiled at her, a real smile that actually reached his eyes. "I think you're very nice."

Her hand was still on his arm, and he placed his own over it, then traced his fingers up her arm toward her shoulder. Even through the wool of her suit jacket she felt the electricity of his touch clear down to the bone.

Her heart was the clapper inside the large bell of her rib cage, thunking back and forth until she was positively dizzy. And yet she couldn't move, couldn't pull away. His eyes mesmerized her, his touch rooted her to the spot, a frozen statue waiting for something to bring her to life.

That something was a kiss.

Most everything Daniel Logan did was calculated down to the last raise of his eyebrows. But this…this was so spontaneous and real, so *not* calculated, that she fell right in line, tilting her head, parting her lips slightly as she tried to suck in a bit more oxygen.

The first contact produced an explosion of sensation. It was a mere brush of his lips on hers, but suddenly her whole body felt alive in a way that was entirely new to her. She could feel every ridge of those oh-so-notorious fingerprints against her skin, feel the course of blood through the veins and arteries of his fingertips.

They shared a breath, and for one insane moment

she wondered if she was about to become the newest member of the mile-high club.

She wanted him. Despite everything she'd just told herself about staying away from "projects," despite the precarious nature of their professional association, despite that she was a prosecutor and he was a bleeding-heart do-gooder, she wanted him.

For a moment it seemed as if he might pull away. She sensed a split second of hesitation, a thread of reasoned thought wrapped in the craziness.

Instead, he kissed her again, less gently this time. His mouth was hot and insistent on hers now, demanding response, demanding surrender.

She wanted to fight the longing that seeped into her every pore, but it was so much easier to give in to feelings, to live in the moment, drowning in sensation and desire and the intimate connection with this dynamic and complex man.

She leaned her head back against the headrest as he took full command of the kiss. He unfastened her seat belt so he could move her closer, then pulled the clip out of her hair so he could dig his fingers into her scalp.

He caressed her ears with his thumbs, sending violent shivers all the way down to her toes.

His tongue darted into her mouth, and Jamie sensed the taste of the fine Scotch, which had somehow transmuted to a pleasant flavor when mingled with Daniel's unique essence. His soap or aftershave—something that smelled like a fresh spring morning after a rain—teased her nose.

Jamie was dimly aware of a noise toward the front of the plane.

"Whoa. Excuse me."

Daniel pulled away abruptly, and Jamie felt as if she'd just come to the surface of a very deep and dark pool. Gasping for breath, she glanced over her shoulder just in time to see Cora retreating into the galley.

She huffed out a nervous laugh as Daniel stared first at the door where Cora had disappeared, then at her, his expression impossible to read. Irritation? Relief? Embarrassment?

Looking for something to do with her suddenly empty hands, she went to work repairing the damage to her hair, finding the discarded clip and finger-combing the unruly strands. "Why do I suddenly feel like a teenager who got caught necking in the backseat of a car?"

"Possibly because we've just done something idiotic, in front of a witness?" Daniel grabbed his forgotten drink and drained it.

Idiotic? How about *earth-moving? Life-altering?* She'd never known any simple kiss to completely shatter her like that one did, but apparently it meant little to Daniel.

Women probably threw themselves at him all the time. Had she thrown herself at him? No, but she certainly hadn't played hard to get.

The way she felt now—it was untenable. She wouldn't

be able to endure his company without thinking about what happened just now.

"Maybe," she said carefully, "it *would* be better if I dealt with one of your associates from now on."

CHAPTER NINE

DANIEL STOOD AND RESUMED his pacing. "Jamie, I apologize. That was totally out of line."

How could he have let go of his control like that? A man's life was at stake, and he *knew* a personal involvement with the prosecutor could jeopardize the fragile common ground they'd found.

"It's all right, Daniel. I'm to blame as much as you." She'd dug a small zippered bag from her briefcase and was busy repairing the damage he'd done to her lipstick. She wouldn't look at him.

He probably had her makeup all over his face, too. He grabbed a paper napkin from the bar and wiped his face. It came back streaked with the rusty-pink shade she wore. It smelled slightly of her teasing scent, too. He folded it carefully and tucked it into his shirt pocket.

"Maybe you're right. Raleigh is very good at negotiating her way around prisons. She can probably smooth over what happened today and arrange another meeting."

Failure didn't sit well with him. In his youth, everything he'd touched had turned golden. Grades and sports came easily. Any woman he wanted was his for the asking. With the exception of his first restaurant, his businesses thrived.

Even after Andreas's murder, all through incarceration and trial, the guilty verdict and the failed appeals, he'd somehow known he would triumph.

True, he wasn't the same man he'd been before prison. But he hadn't lost his drive, and when he was passionate about something, he applied himself and made it happen.

Though his father had died when Project Justice was in its infancy, Daniel had single-handedly molded it into the vision they'd shared, as a tribute to the man who had never lost faith in him. He was accustomed to winning, even if he had lost the feeling of joy he used to have.

This business of failure didn't feel good.

"I'll still be involved," he said. Because if he wasn't involved, how else was he going to make sure the person who framed him paid the price for his crime? "But day to day, you'll be dealing with Raleigh. I'll bring her up to speed as quickly as possible."

"Whatever you think is best." She didn't sound any happier than he felt about it.

Daniel made his way forward and tapped on the galley door. Cora opened it. "Yes?"

"Coast is clear."

Cora smiled nervously and followed him into the main cabin. "I was just going to ask if you folks wanted a snack."

"I'm not really very hungry, thank you, Cora. Jamie?"

"I'm starving," she admitted.

Hmm. Usually he had to force-feed her.

Cora disappeared once again into the galley, which Daniel knew was fully equipped to facilitate the preparation of gourmet meals for up to ten people.

But Cora, who was fully capable of said gourmet meal, instead produced two fancy cloth bags that bore the logo of AirKitchens, handing one to each of them.

Daniel gave Cora a questioning look. "Airline food?"

"Jillian said for such a short flight, I shouldn't go to the bother of cooking. Did I do the wrong thing?"

"No, this is fine, Cora," he said soothingly.

Jillian again. If she didn't curb this jealous streak of hers, she was going to end up unemployed, never mind her long history with the family.

"Are you set for beverages?" Cora asked.

"Yes. Thanks again."

She quietly retreated.

Daniel sat across from Jamie, pulled out a tray table and examined the contents of the bag. Some kind of sandwich, bag of chips, a brownie and apple juice.

Jamie dumped out her bag and went straight for the brownie. She ate it as if she hadn't had chocolate in years. Bolting down a brownie was so unlike her usual behavior that he had to laugh.

"You might think a lot of Chef Claude's tiramisu,"

she said between bites, "but this brownie is the best thing I've ever eaten."

Maybe it was the aftereffect of being inside the prison walls. Everyone tended to take freedom for granted until they were forced to consider what the lack of it meant.

Or maybe she was substituting chocolate for sex.

He pulled at the cellophane around the brownie and stuffed some of the dessert into his mouth. Not bad for airplane food. But certainly no substitute for having Jamie naked and writhing beneath him.

God, he would miss her.

JAMIE MANAGED TO HOLD HERSELF together throughout the rest of the short flight. She kept herself busy gobbling down every single bite of the prefab lunch, despite the fact she'd eaten a Danish only a short time earlier. Her sudden ravenous appetite was as baffling as it was impossible to ignore.

She wondered what prisoners on death row got to eat. Like hospital food, she imagined, only worse. Christopher would eat alone, she imagined, just as he did everything else.

After they landed, Jamie was surprised to find two cars waiting to shuttle them off to their separate destinations. Her heart sank; she'd been counting on those last few minutes, riding in the limo together, to mentally say her goodbyes to Daniel.

Working on this case with him had stimulated her in every way—physically, intellectually, emotionally. She hadn't realized what she'd been missing, slaving away in her little cubicle at the D.A.'s office, methodically clearing cases, pleading them out when she could, going to trial when she had to.

Most of them were cut-and-paste cases. An intriguing murder, like ones Daniel and Christopher had been charged with, came along very rarely in a prosecutor's life.

She didn't want Daniel to hand the case over to someone else. But she also didn't want to subject him to any more of the emotional trauma he'd gone through today.

At some point, Daniel might actually be required to testify before a judge, depending on what they found and how they found it—especially if she managed to conclusively tie the two cases together.

"I've enjoyed getting to know you, Jamie," Daniel said. "We'll talk again soon. Meanwhile, expect to hear from Raleigh."

"All right. I've enjoyed getting to know you, too." At least those parts of him he was willing to show her. He kept a lot of himself hidden away.

He took her hand and clasped it between his. "Take care, okay?"

"Yeah. You, too." Her voice cracked, giving her away.

"This way, Ms. McNair." Randall led her toward the Bentley. "Celeste will drive you home."

"Celeste? Who is she?"

"One of Daniel's most trusted employees. Don't let appearances fool you. You'll be safe with her."

What was that supposed to mean?

Though Randall tried to open the Bentley's back door, Jamie climbed into the passenger seat. "I've had enough *Lifestyles of the Rich and Famous* today, so don't argue with me."

"Wouldn't dream of it."

He made sure she was safely inside and closed her door. Only then did she look over at her new driver.

Good night. The woman was well into her seventies, judging from all the creases in her face and the wild, gray hair, which she'd tried and failed to tame with a series of little-girl barrettes. She wore a blousy top splashed with loud red poinsettias and green leggings tucked into black boots that reached above her knees.

"Hello, dear. I'm Celeste Boggs, office manager and head of security at Project Justice." With that, one of those amazing boots hit the gas, and the Bentley shot forward like a rocket. "Woo-hoo, always wanted to drive me one of these."

Jamie grabbed on to the door handle. "It sounds like you have a lot of responsibility at Project Justice."

"The place would fall apart without me."

"I'm sorry to have taken you away from your normal job, then."

"It's no problem. In fact, I volunteered. I wanted to see firsthand the woman who got Daniel off his estate. Twice in a week's time."

Jamie wasn't sure if Celeste approved or not. She drove 70 mph down the farm-to-market road that led from the airport to the freeway and whooped every time the Bentley hit a bump and nearly became airborne.

"Tell the truth now," Celeste said. "Are you and Daniel doin' the horizontal mambo?"

"What? No! In fact, I probably won't be seeing him again."

"Really." Celeste sounded as if she didn't believe Jamie.

"He's handing over our project to another person, so we won't be working together anymore. It wasn't working out."

"So you're dropping him like a hot rock?"

Jamie was startled by Celeste's hostility. "I'm not 'dropping' him. It was his decision to pull back." Well, a mutual decision, anyway.

"So you're not working together anymore. Does that mean you can't see him anymore?"

"Celeste, we aren't personally involved."

"Huh, you might not think you are. But these last couple of weeks, Daniel's been a completely different man."

"Different…how?" she felt compelled to ask.

"Alive. Oh, technically he was alive before. Walking, talking, breathing, letting Skeletor move him around like a piece on a chessboard."

"Skeletor?"

"Jillian, I mean. Girl could use some meat on her

bones, that's all," Celeste muttered. "But he was more like a walking corpse. Just going through the motions of living.

"But since he met you—he's a different man. He *cares* about stuff now. He smiles, he's excited, he's like the old Daniel. You walk out of his life, he'll go back to being corpse man again."

Jamie was flabbergasted. Surely Celeste was exaggerating. How much did she even see of Daniel?

"I think it's working on the case that has, er, exhilarated him," Jamie said carefully. "He'll still be involved, just not running the show."

"I beg to disagree. It's you. He needs a real woman in his life. Why not you?"

Jamie screamed as Celeste swerved to avoid a rabbit that dashed across the road. "Would you like to hear the reasons alphabetically or in order of importance?"

"A lot of women would kill to be in your position."

"That's not a good enough reason to want a relationship." She softened when she recognized the look of worry and concern on Celeste's face. "Look, it's not that I don't think Daniel is a good man. But for many reasons, pursuing a relationship with him would be… unwise. What if it didn't work out?"

"That's the risk in any relationship, isn't it?" Celeste sounded quite sane all of a sudden.

"But the fallout…with Daniel…" She stopped short of pointing out that Celeste's boss had issues. And she didn't want to become one of them.

"Do you consider him a friend?" Celeste asked.

"Yes." She'd realized that just today.

"If you don't want to date him, he could use a friend. He doesn't have many, you know. It's hard for someone in his position to make friends. Everybody wants something from him. Or they're afraid of offending him."

"He has you. And Randall, and Cora and Claude, and all the people at Project Justice. He holds you all in such high esteem."

"I do count Daniel as a friend. But I'm also his employee. We're not equals. You see yourself as his equal, and that's rare."

She didn't want to come out and tell Celeste that after such a mind-bending kiss, she didn't think she could be "just friends" with Daniel.

"It's not my decision to make. If Daniel wants any further dealings with me, he has my phone number."

"And he'll be too proud to dial it."

DANIEL HAD NEVER APPRECIATED his home as much as he did that day, as Randall drove him through the wrought-iron gate into the safety of his estate.

"You look awful," Jillian said bluntly as he entered through the garage door. "I know you can't reveal too much about an open case, but did it go well?"

Surely she'd been able to tell by his demeanor that things hadn't gone well. "No, I'm afraid it was a spectacular failure."

"I'm sorry to hear that."

"No, you're not."

She looked at him sharply. "Excuse me? Of course I'm sorry. Why would I want you to fail?"

"Maybe so you can prove you were right and I was wrong? That I shouldn't have left the estate, especially without you, because I wasn't ready."

He yanked off his jacket and handed it to her out of habit.

"Are you going to tell me what happened?"

"I had a….a panic attack." Might as well call a spade a spade. "I never saw my client because I couldn't walk into the prison."

"Oh, Daniel. I'm sorry."

"I've put the whole case in jeopardy."

"I'm sure you're exaggerating. Have you had lunch? Claude has been working on something *très mystérieuse* this morning, and it smells divine."

"I had a sandwich on the plane." He couldn't remember much about the lunch. His mind was too full of kissing Jamie.

"Then why don't I schedule a massage this afternoon."

It was tempting to let Jillian take over. But Jillian's overfunctioning had been his crutch for too long. If today had taught him one lesson, it was that he needed to take back control of his life.

"I have work to do."

"Work. That reminds me—someone called from

Project Justice. Lab results or something—she said it was important."

"*Someone* called? You didn't happen to catch a name?" What was wrong with Jillian? Normally she could quote verbatim from memory any message she'd taken for him.

"I wrote it down. It's on your desk."

It could be a call from one of his people, just giving him a progress report on another case. Jamie had sent everything to PrakTech Labs. They would report any results directly to her. But Beth McClelland, head of the Project Justice lab, had a mole at PrakTech who would report directly to her.

Why hadn't Jillian immediately forwarded the information to his phone? He could have returned the call during the drive. Unless she was trying to shield him from unhappy news?

Now that he knew, or at least suspected, that Jillian had feelings for him, he questioned her motives in everything. All the more reason to transfer her away from the estate.

As Daniel passed through the kitchen, he caught the scent of Claude's creations—onion and garlic and delicate spices he couldn't even identify floated lightly in the air. Claude was in full regalia today, with apron and tall hat, a dishcloth draped over each shoulder.

"What are you up to?" Daniel asked.

"Trying new recipes for the Christmas party. Jillian

says we are having it here. My reputation is at stake. I have to wow your guests."

Daniel didn't want to burst Claude's bubble, but his Project Justice parties were only a bunch of ex-cops and lawyers. He could serve most of them day-old burritos and Mountain Dew and they'd be happy.

"I'm sure whatever you serve, everyone will be impressed," Daniel said, because Claude's ego needed stroking on a regular basis. When they'd worked together at their restaurant, Le Bistro, nothing made him happier than when a diner made the special effort to personally compliment him on the dishes he prepared. When they'd gotten a good write-up in *Food* magazine, he'd been nearly apoplectic with joy.

It had to be a little bit different working in a private home. Though Claude was compensated well, this was a much more private life. Maybe Daniel could ask Griffin Benedict, his newest agent and a former journalist, to write up a story about the office party—with special emphasis on the food—and submit it to the local society rag. The magazine had asked numerous times to do a feature story on him or his home—anything—and he'd always declined.

Both Claude and Jillian would get a kick out of that.

"Smells great. Carry on."

Claude, his hands busy separating thin sheets of phyllo dough, nodded, and Daniel headed straight down to his office, Jillian following him with a rundown of his afternoon schedule.

She had, indeed, left a sticky note on his desk. Very old-school of her. He had a complex schedule software program that she normally used to coordinate phone calls and messages.

He shook his head.

"Jillian," Daniel said, "call Raleigh and make an appointment with her. Set aside at least an hour. Tell her I'm handing over the Christopher Gables case to her."

"You are? Really? Why?"

"Just do it, okay?" She knew why. He'd just told her a few minutes ago. His reaction to being near a prison had jeopardized the case, and Jillian knew as well as anyone how important these wrongly imprisoned men and women were to him.

Did she want him to go over it again? So she could comfort him?

The message was indeed from Beth.

He donned his Bluetooth earpiece, then clicked the link on his computer that would put in a call directly to the lab.

"Beth. What's up?"

"We've got a match."

His blood pounded inside his ears. "Between the two crime scenes? Andreas Musto and Frank Sissom?" he clarified, just to be sure.

"Yes. An unidentified body-fluid sample found on

Musto's shirt matched an unidentified saliva sample found on Sissom's apron."

Daniel came out of his chair. "But no matches in the database?"

"Those results aren't in yet."

"Okay. Thanks, Beth."

Still, this was huge. The two cases were definitely connected.

Christopher Gables had been a twenty-one-year-old college senior at Kansas State University at the time of Andreas's murder. He had no conceivable connection to that case.

Finally, they had a viable suspect for both murders. As yet unidentified, but that would come.

If there was a match, Daniel would finally have the name of the man who had brutally murdered his friend and framed Daniel. They could present their evidence to the Harris County sheriff's department and pressure them to reopen the case.

But Daniel had much swifter justice in mind.

The next thing he did, as soon as he disconnected from talking with Beth, was to dial Jamie's number.

Of all the people in the world, she was the one he wanted to share the news with.

"Daniel?"

"Jamie. Could you come over right away?"

"I just got home."

"This is important. I have news. I can call Celeste, have her turn around—"

"Good God, no, that woman is a menace to drivers everywhere. I can take my own car."

He didn't understand the reason for the sharpness he heard in her voice, but just now he didn't care. He would straighten everything out when she got here.

He hadn't ruined the case after all. They now had a strong piece of physical evidence that would reopen both cases.

He picked up the framed portrait of his parents, the only nonfunctional object he allowed on his desk. "Dad, we're on our way. I'm going to find the animal who derailed my life. And I'm going to personally see that justice is done this time."

His office door opened a crack and Jillian poked her head in. "Oh. I thought you were on the phone."

Daniel set the picture down. "What is it?"

"Raleigh is in court, and she'll be there all day. Soonest she can get you in is probably tomorrow."

"That's okay, never mind." He wasn't going to let go of this case, not now. Not when victory was so close. If he handed it over to Raleigh, he would have no more reason to see Jamie.

And he wanted reasons—lots of reasons—to see her.

He might have miscalculated, summoning her as if she had no choice in the matter. Old habits were hard to break. But he had to stop thinking of Jamie as someone he could manipulate or use for his own purposes.

"Jamie is on her way over," he told Jillian. "Send her into the library when she arrives."

"You just spent all morning with her."

"Yeah, so…?"

"Doesn't she have a job?"

"She has the day off. Jillian, I know you don't like her, but I don't appreciate your questioning me every time I schedule an appointment with her. She is a crucial part of the puzzle with the case I'm working on."

"Mmm. Sorry."

"How are the plans for the holiday party coming along?" he asked, hoping to distract her from her negative thoughts.

She smiled. "Fabulous. The decorations are arriving today, everything except the ice sculptures. By Friday, this place is going to look like a winter wonderland. We're going to have a snow machine and sleigh rides."

Ice sculptures? Sleigh rides? Oh, God help him. Well, maybe his people would like the novelty. They all worked so hard. One evening of fantasy might be appreciated.

By the time Jamie arrived, Daniel was waiting in the library. Anxious to be out of the suit and tie—which still, in his mind, smelled like prison—he'd changed into a pair of worn jeans and a sweater. He'd built a fire—the temperature outside was down in the fifties, cold enough to justify a warm blaze, he figured—and Claude had sent a plate full of appetizers for him to sample and approve for the party.

Not that he really cared; they would all be good. But the party had become a big deal to his staff, so he would humor them.

He tossed a stuffed mushroom to Tucker, who was watching intently but was too well trained to beg.

When the door opened and Jillian ushered Jamie in, he shot out of his chair.

She really had just gotten home when he called, apparently, because she hadn't even changed out of her suit. He felt a little underdressed.

"Do you need anything, Daniel?" Jillian asked sweetly.

"No, thanks. In fact, take the rest of the day off." Her hovering had become a bit tiresome.

"Thank you." She didn't sound grateful at all.

"Daniel, what's this about?" Jamie asked when they were alone. "I don't like games."

He frowned. "I didn't mean for it to be a game. But it's good news. Too good for the phone."

"What?"

"The lab found a DNA match between the two murders. They're definitely linked."

For a moment, she stood there looking stunned. "So we're back to the serial-killer idea?" she asked dubiously.

"All I know is, the two cases are definitely linked, and by more than the coincidence of metal shavings. Gables was a college kid halfway across the country at the time of the first murder, and I can prove it. He was sitting for a final exam in a Shakespeare class. He has no possible connection. Someone else committed both crimes."

"Holy crap."

This wasn't the reaction he'd hoped for. "I thought you'd be happy."

"Happy that the client I prosecuted and put on death row is innocent?" She collapsed into the sofa and idly petted Tucker, who looked worried. The dog was amazingly attuned to the feelings of people around him.

"You've known this was a possibility for a long time. You said you wanted answers."

"I did want answers. I thought they'd be different. I wanted proof that I did the right thing."

Daniel realized he hadn't thought this through. He'd been so focused on the outcome *he* wanted, he'd forgotten the implications for Jamie.

He sat down beside her on the sofa. "Listen, Jamie. You've done an enormously courageous thing. Yes, you prosecuted the wrong man. But that's because someone framed Christopher. Someone planted evidence. You can't be blamed—"

"Of course I can be blamed. You don't think Chubb will make me the sacrificial lamb? I'll lose my job. By the time he's done with me, I won't be able to get work as a prosecutor anywhere in the country."

"Let's look at the bigger picture. We are going to right a cruel injustice. We're going to save a man's life. And we are perilously close to finding the actual murderer in two high-profile, now-unsolved cases."

"How do you figure that?"

"We've got his DNA. If we have to get samples from every person in the country, we'll find a match. You don't think Chubb would like that? If you brought him a person who'd almost gotten away with two brutal murders?"

"Daniel, you're forgetting. I won't be a part of that. Once we show that Christopher didn't kill anyone, my role in this is over."

"No. I won't accept that."

She sat up straighter and looked at him, suddenly steely-eyed. "Yes, Daniel, you will have to accept that. There are some things in this world that your money can't buy, and I'm one of them."

"Did I say anything about money?"

"It's implied. You're so used to getting your way, and everyone in our life is so eager to please you that you forget other people have free will."

"Let me rephrase, then. I don't accept that you don't *want* to keep going. To find the man who took two lives and ruined two others... That doesn't excite you?"

She took her time answering. "I would be pleased to prosecute that man as part of my job. But, for me, it's not personal."

Daniel had a hard time understanding how these life-or-death issues could *not* be personal. But he had to tread carefully here. If Jamie figured out what his true intent was, she would find a way to stop him.

"So this case is nothing personal? Just business?"

She nodded curtly.

"What was that kiss all about then?" Just saying the word *kiss* caused every part of Daniel's body to tighten. They were in the middle of an argument, and all he wanted to do was kiss her again. And again.

Jamie, her gaze locked with his, licked her lips and swallowed. "Th-that kiss is immaterial to this discussion. We were talking about the justice system. Our work."

She made perfect sense. Yet somehow Daniel had gotten the whole thing mixed up in his mind. If he could find closure, check this one item off his list, he could move on to other things.

To Jamie.

The news about the DNA had given him real hope for the first time in a very long time. For Jamie, the stakes were professional. For him, they were very, very personal. And she didn't get it.

"You're right. Immaterial. Completely out of line for me to even bring it up." With that, he leaned in and kissed her again.

CHAPTER TEN

THOUGH EVERY PART OF HER BODY wanted to melt into a pool of surrender, she pulled back. "Daniel…"

"I want you, Jamie. You want the same thing. I can see it in your eyes. I can feel it on your lips."

"That doesn't make it…"

He kissed her again, harder this time, placing his hands on her shoulders and pressing her against the back of the sofa. A delicious lethargy stole over her body as the kiss intoxicated her.

Yes, he was right, she did want him.

After a few moments, or maybe it was a few minutes, he came up for air. "You were saying?"

She had to search her beleaguered brain for her argument. "Mutual desire…doesn't justify…"

"We're both single…" *Kiss* "…unattached…" *Kiss* "…consenting…" *Kiss.*

Why not? She sensed there was a good reason to resist Daniel's appeal, but she couldn't come up with it.

"Jamie." He whispered against her ear. "I haven't felt

this good about anything in years. It feels *right*. I want to celebrate. I want to make love to you."

Jamie's cynical side clamored for attention. He was manipulating her again. Like most men when they wanted something, they said whatever it took to get their way.

But somehow none of that seemed to matter. She wanted to be with him at least as badly as he wanted her.

She didn't kid herself that he was serious about her. Lowly county prosecutors from the wrong side of the tracks didn't become the girlfriends of billionaire oil tycoons except in fairy tales.

But as Daniel nibbled on her earlobe, waiting for a yes or no from her, she didn't care much what the future held. She'd been attracted to Daniel from the first time she'd seen him lying naked on that massage table, and her hunger for the man had done nothing but build.

It *did* feel right. For this moment, anyway.

"Daniel?"

He stilled, tense, waiting for her to reject him. "Yes?"

"Is the door locked?"

"My staff knows better than to walk in here when I'm in a meeting. Not unless the house is on fire."

"I don't care. Lock it."

"Happy to." Tucker followed him, and he nudged the dog out the door before locking it. Then he returned to

Jamie and put his arms around her. "Is that a yes, dear Jamie?"

"It is." Something still nagged at her, but she shoved it aside. Daniel Logan was going to make love to her, and she was damn well going to enjoy it.

He kissed her neck and she wiggled with anticipation. Committed, now, she was downright eager.

"Are you protected?" he asked almost casually as he deftly unbuttoned her blouse with one hand and she slid farther and farther down until she was nearly horizontal on the buttery-soft leather sofa.

Of course he would have to ask. A man in his position didn't risk paying astronomical child support to some enterprising young lady.

"Yes." At the urging of her father years ago, she'd gotten an IUD so she didn't have to worry about birth control.

One careless moment could derail your whole career.

She'd never been sure why he felt that way, since her conception hadn't been even a speed bump in his career, unless an occasional birthday gift… *Damn.*

Her father. That was the thing that was bothering her. Daniel still didn't know her relationship to the man who had sent him to death row.

Daniel had her shirt all the way unbuttoned and was working on the front clasp of her bra.

"Daniel. Daniel, wait. I have to tell you something."

His fingers went still. "It can wait. Can't it?"

He was right. If she brought up the subject of her father right now, it would kill the mood completely. "Never mind. It's not important." At least, it didn't seem very important in this context.

What difference did it really make that her father had prosecuted Daniel? She'd never been close to her father. She'd had only a handful of face-to-face meetings with him, during which he preached and she absorbed what she perceived as his wisdom. She was in no way directly connected to the miscarriage of justice that had put Daniel away.

She smiled, made herself relax again.

Why was she fighting this so hard? As Daniel said, they were two consenting adults and there was no ethical or moral reason they couldn't make love.

She sat up and stripped off her blouse and jacket at the same time. Her bra followed. Daniel stared at her with hungry eyes, like a kid who'd just won the biggest stuffed animal at the carnival.

"Can I touch?" he asked almost shyly.

She wondered if she was his first since prison. If so, he'd hardly been more than a kid the last time he'd been with a woman. She took his hand and guided it to her breast. The muscles of her abdomen spasmed as he touched her.

"You're so beautiful," he said reverently.

A deer head mounted over the fireplace seemed to be looking at her accusingly. She closed her eyes and shut out all distractions, focusing on the feel of his hand on her breast, his thumb caressing her nipple.

For the second time that day, he pulled the clip out of her hair and dug his fingers through it, massaging her scalp as he massaged her breast.

Jamie slid her feet out of her shoes and reached for the side zipper of her pants. She wanted to be naked, to open herself completely. She wanted to feel the texture of his skin, feel the heat of it touching her.

"I don't want to let go of you long enough to get undressed," he said. "Isn't that insane? But I'm afraid you'll evaporate."

"I'm here, Daniel, and I'm not going anywhere."

He let go of her to quickly unbutton his shirt and peel it off, revealing a chest that was tanned to a golden brown. The skin was smooth, with just a light dusting of hair at the center.

His jeans came next. Her mouth went dry as he shoved them down his legs, revealing a pair of navy boxer briefs that showed every inch of the extent of his desire for her.

Then the underwear was gone, too, and she couldn't take her eyes off his beautiful male anatomy, standing proudly, ripe for her taking.

Suddenly, more than anything, she wanted to take him in her mouth and shower her attention on him. She'd heard men preferred the activity over all others, because it was the only time a woman's attention was focused solely on his pleasure, forsaking her own.

She wouldn't be forsaking anything. Without any conscious decision she sat up straighter, reached for him, placed her hands on his hip bones and urge him to stand in front of her.

"What… Oh."

Jamie took him into her mouth, exploring him from the base of his shaft to the tip with her eager, curious tongue and lips while he filled his hands with handfuls of her hair.

"Um, Jamie…" The words came out on a groan and she realized he was fighting for control. "I want to be inside…"

She released him. "Yes. Yes, I want that, too." Their first time, perhaps their only time, she wanted him to climax inside her.

Jamie raised her hips from the sofa just long enough to shuck her pants and panties, kicking them out of the way as she grabbed Daniel's wrist and pulled him down on top of her.

His weight crushed her and she loved it, feeling pinned and helpless for a few seconds as he adjusted their positions, insinuating himself between her legs.

"I'm not hurting you…?"

"No. Oh, Daniel, please. Now."

Even before he entered her, heat pooled between her legs and her skin tingled all over, forecasting what she knew was going to be an explosive orgasm.

She threw one leg over the back of the sofa, opening herself to him. She was wet and ready for him, her whole body throbbing with need. Reaching between their bodies, she grasped his erection. They both groaned as she guided him into her. But it wasn't as if he couldn't find her on his own. He pushed inside, paused, pushed deeper, paused.

She was hyperventilating, and she forced herself to clamp her mouth shut, breathing through her nose as he took possession of her, sheathing himself even more deeply, and she spread her legs wider to give him full access.

He was nearly nose to nose with her, and he looked deeply into her eyes. "Jamie."

That one word was a powerful aphrodisiac. It said he knew to whom he was making love, that she wasn't some interchangeable collection of female body parts.

He withdrew almost all the way until she whimpered, then plunged inside again, his stroke hard and swift this time. After a few moments, unless she'd lost track of time altogether, he paused again, still struggling for control and driving her to the brink of insanity.

She deliberately moved against him.

"No wiggling."

"Do that again, Daniel."

"Only if you want this to end way too soon."

She never wanted it to end. "Then take your time." Still, he repeated the long withdraw, and again plunged inside until it felt as if he were reaching down into her core and touching parts of her psyche that had lain dormant her whole life until now. Frothy emotions bubbled up inside her, uncontrollable yet strangely pleasant.

Eventually he found the control he'd been striving for and began to stroke her in earnest, working her into a frenzy.

This wasn't sex. It was a slow stairway to heaven, not even on the same plane as any encounters in her past.

Daniel's strokes intensified, and what had started as a leisurely stroll turned into an Olympic sprint. When she finally couldn't take the tension a moment longer she relaxed her body with a whimper, giving over complete control.

The pleasure was the most intense she'd ever felt as tingles rippled from her core outward in wave after crashing wave.

Daniel released the grip on his self-control and tensed, his whole body rigid. Jamie wrapped her arms and legs around him, practically absorbing his climax along with him.

Gradually she became aware of their physical surroundings again—the feel of the leather against her naked bottom, the afternoon's winter light spilling through the blinds and that blasted deer head looking down on her.

Idiot. What have you done?

Their bodies were slick with sweat, as if they'd just run a marathon. Physically she was exhausted, spent down to the last penny. She wondered how in the world she would put her clothes on and stroll out of this room as if nothing had happened.

But she would. Gossip about her and Daniel would get back to her office like wildfire and kill her career. If anything was left of her career.

Daniel eased himself off her, swinging her legs over the side of the sofa, sitting down, then pulling her against him.

Cuddling. Nice touch.

"You wanted to tell me something?"

Of course he would remember. "It was good for me, too."

He laughed. "Sorry. But I was rude to put you off so abruptly. It seemed like it was important to you and my lust got the better of my manners."

Now wasn't the time. "It wasn't important."

Maybe he didn't have to know. If she didn't tell him, no one else would. No one knew.

"Would you mind if I dressed?" she asked. "I feel really odd, knowing your house is crawling with servants. I mean, what if the house really does catch fire and someone has to run in here to save our lives?"

"You get used to servants. But go ahead. As long as I can watch."

She felt slightly self-conscious—which was ridiculous, given what they'd just shared—as she pulled on panties and bra, pants, shirt, all while Daniel observed appreciatively.

"Not *quite* as interesting going on as they were coming off, but not bad."

When she was dressed, he quickly donned his own clothes, his movements graceful and economical. He was right, it was fun to watch.

"Now what?" she asked. She had no expectations. Really, none.

"I have a luxurious apartment on the third floor where I install all my lovers. You'll have everything you need, and your only responsibility will be to please me."

The shock must have showed on her face, because he laughed. "Jamie. God, what you must think of me. I'm kidding. You act like I have all the answers, and I haven't got a clue. I was hoping you'd tell me."

"Unfortunately, I think we have to pretend this never happened. We're professionally involved." Why was she saying this? Was she making a preemptive strike so he couldn't reject her first? She didn't want to go back to their previous amicable but strained way of being around each other.

But lying down in the path of a herd of runaway cattle wasn't her style, either.

The look he gave her was inscrutable. "Fine. Once you get official word of the DNA results, we'll decide together how to proceed."

"Okay, but keep in mind, if you want me publicly connected to this thing, I'll soon be a disgraced and jobless former prosecutor."

He shook his head. "Don't be so sure. If there's

anything I can do to shore up your professional reputation, I'll do it. But presented in the right light, I think you can come up smelling like roses. You took the courageous step to right an injustice, and you'll catch a serial killer in the bargain."

It sounded good when he put it that way.

"I'll wait to hear from you."

Jamie went into the half bath off the library to repair her appearance. Thank God she'd tucked a hairbrush and her travel makeup bag into her purse.

She could fix the wild-looking hair and the smeared lipstick and straighten her clothes, but she couldn't take the roses out of her cheeks. Try as she might, when she looked in the mirror, she still looked like a woman who'd just enjoyed an afternoon of passion.

"One more thing," Daniel said when she rejoined him. He was still barefoot and his hair was mussed from her digging her fingers through it.

In fact, he looked so good that she could easily have jumped him again—if she'd been a woman of little self-control.

"Yes, what is it?"

"Can you come to the holiday party?"

"Isn't it just for the Project Justice employees?"

"And their families, close friends and a few key associates. You qualify."

As a friend or key associate?

"If it's important to you. Jillian won't like your adding

me to the guest list. She's probably planned a sit-down dinner with seating arrangements."

"Jillian is my employee. She'll deal with it."

Jamie smiled. "All right. I'll come, then." It might be difficult and slightly awkward, but how could she say no to the man who had just pleasured her so fiercely?

JAMIE GOT TO WORK EARLY the next day, hoping to make some sense of her in-box and her phone messages before her official workday began. But the first thing she saw was a note smack in the middle of her desk. It was written in angry capital letters on Winston Chubb's personal notepaper: SEE ME.

That really didn't sound good.

He wasn't in yet, so Jamie had a few minutes to get worked up about what he wanted. Had he found out about her consorting with Daniel?

I've done nothing wrong. She'd investigated on her own time, off the county payroll, and she'd taken no official action.

But she'd gone directly against what her boss had told her to do. Winston would see it as a frontal assault to his authority, and it would not be pretty.

When she heard his voice from the hallway, floating over the partitions into her tiny cubicle office, her stomach flipped. She had to get this over with.

She made sure her clothes were straight and she didn't have lipstick on her teeth. Then she charged off to his office, ready to defend her actions.

"He wanted to see me right away," she explained to Alice, Winston's admin.

"Go on back," Alice said with an uncharacteristic smile and wink, as if she knew something Jamie didn't know.

Jamie tapped on Winston's door, and he summoned her inside.

"Ah, Jamie. Just who I wanted to see. Have a seat."

He was smiling. Why was he smiling? Surely he wouldn't take that much pleasure in firing her.

"As you know, Jamie, this is my last term as Harris County district attorney. I'll be retiring in May."

"In May? Your term isn't up until September."

"I have personal reasons for leaving office early, but that's immaterial. The county already has a special election scheduled for April, and the people are going to vote in a new D.A. I'm thinking that person should be you."

Oh, boy. This really wasn't what she'd expected.

"You look surprised."

"To say the least. When you mentioned the possibility before, I assumed you meant far into the future."

"With my endorsement, you'd be a shoo-in. You're a little young for the job, I'll admit, and you and I have had our run-ins, but when I look around this office, you're the one who's most capable of doing the job."

"I'm flattered." For a few seconds, she let herself fantasize about it. Harris County District Attorney Jamie McNair. Her father would be so proud...

No, her father wouldn't give a rat's ass. It was time for her to concede that the man had been a narcissist, and anything that didn't directly concern him didn't make a blip on his personal radar screen. His only reason for giving her career advice was so that she could be a reflection of him, a "mini-me" he could someday brag about to his big-shot friends, if she distinguished herself.

"Good. I've set up a meeting with my campaign people—they're ready to gear up the 'Jamie McNair for District Attorney' machine as soon as you sign on the dotted line. Are you free on Friday after work?"

Friday evening was Daniel's party. Oh, who was she kidding? She couldn't even consider running for D.A., not when a big fat PR nightmare was about to hit the fan.

"Winston, I'm honored, really. But there's something you need to know, and you won't like it."

His eyebrows flew up. "What? Is there a skeleton in your closet I don't know about? Child out of wedlock? Illicit affair with the county sheriff?"

He was kidding, because he believed her to be of sterling character. She was about to change his mind.

"I prosecuted an innocent man and sent him to death row."

"Oh, God, not the Christopher Gables thing. Is Project Justice actually pursuing that case?"

"Yes, and I'm afraid they've come up with some definitive evidence. DNA links the murder of Frank

Sissom with another similar crime for which Gables is in no way connected, and for which he has an ironclad alibi."

"And you know this...how?" he asked suspiciously.

"I've been working with Project Justice during my off hours. I had to know, Winston. I had to know if Gables was innocent. And I firmly believe he is."

"You're going to trash the reputation of this office—*my* reputation—because you were curious? Is that how you want me to leave office? Disgraced?"

"It's my reputation. I take full responsibility."

"You certainly better." He stood up, and for one insane moment she thought he was going to leap across his desk and go for her throat.

"We could take a courageous stand," she said in one last-ditch effort to get him to understand. "We made a mistake. We're taking responsibility for it and righting an injustice. And we may actually be able to bring the real killer—in two murder cases—to justice."

"*You* made a mistake," he corrected her. "I told you to block Project Justice, and you've assisted them instead. I'll expect your letter of resignation on my desk by noon."

"You don't even want to see how this plays out?"

"I already know. We're going to look bad, the media is going to have a field day and my last days in office are going to be a living hell. Thank you, Ms. McNair."

Fine, if that was how he wanted to view the situation.

She stood. "I've done nothing wrong and I won't resign. You'll have to fire me."

"Yes, that would look better. Consider it done."

CHAPTER ELEVEN

DANIEL HAD SO MUCH ENERGY, he couldn't stay inside. Giving the briefest of excuses to Jillian, he set off for the stables, intending to give Laramie as well as himself some exercise.

Usually he grabbed a golf cart for transportation to the stables, but today he walked—partly to discourage Jillian from following him, which she was inclined to do if she felt he was neglecting some portion of the schedule she arranged for him.

She wouldn't be able to negotiate the wet grass in the high-heeled shoes she perpetually wore.

He was only now beginning to see the degree to which he had allowed Jillian to dictate his life. He'd thought of it as a convenience—one of the privileges his money afforded him. But it had become a weakness.

He had imagined that his lifestyle gave him complete control. But he'd turned over control to everybody else. Even his meals were planned by Claude. Oh, sure, he could request something, but when it came right down to it, Claude cooked what Claude wanted to cook.

Things needed to change, and watching Jamie walk out his front door had convinced him of that. She had used their professional association as an excuse for pulling back. But that wasn't why she couldn't embrace the idea of the two of them together. He'd asked her point-blank what she wanted to happen next, and she'd backed away as quickly as she could.

His theory was, she couldn't see herself fitting into his life, as it currently stood. He never left the estate—well, very rarely, and only if sorely pressed. He had servants doing everything for him. He had polo ponies for pets. He had no social life, no friends except the ones on his payroll.

He had panic attacks when he couldn't control things around him, like at the prison. He hadn't wanted to put a name on what had happened at the Conklin Unit, but that's what it was.

He was *paranoid*.

Well, no more. Things were going to change. He was going to start living a more normal life. And somehow, he was going to convince Jamie McNair that she ought to be a part of it.

He knew it would be difficult. After his disastrous trip to north Texas, the very idea of getting in a car and driving off the estate made him queasy. But whatever it took—therapy or hiring a coach, maybe convincing Randall to push him—he'd do it.

Laramie was grazing in a small paddock off the stable. Daniel grabbed a handful of oats and lured the animal to him, then looped a halter around his head and led him into the barn. He bridled the gelding, but didn't bother with a saddle.

When he'd been a kid, he'd had a pony that he loved to ride bareback all over the estate.

He jumped onto Laramie's back with no saddle, and the horse just stood there and turned his head as if to say, *What are you doing?* But Daniel nudged him with the lightest of kicks to the horse's flanks, and he moved forward, obedient beast that he was.

They rode around the estate, walking at first, then cantering and finally at a full-out gallop, dodging trees and jumping walls, and—though not on purpose— trampling a flower bed. Daniel hugged the horse's barrel-shaped body with his knees and leaned low over his neck, guiding him more with his thoughts than the bridle.

He felt truly free.

Daniel rode hard until he was gasping with exhilaration and the horse was lathered with sweat. After cooling him down with a few minutes of walking he returned to the barn, intending to give the horse a rubdown himself rather than turn him over to a groom.

Instead, he found…Jillian. She'd taken the golf cart and followed him after all.

"Have you gone insane?" she asked.

"What? I can't ride my own horse?"

"He's a polo pony. You were riding him like he was a wild mustang."

"And it was a helluva lot of fun, too, wasn't it, fella?"

He gave the horse a pat and led him into his stall, placing a blanket over him so he wouldn't get chilled.

Luis, his groom, appeared out of nowhere. Sometimes Daniel didn't appreciate how truly skilled his staff was—there when he needed them, invisible when he didn't.

"I'll take him," Luis offered.

"No, that's all right. I got him all sweaty, I'll rub him down. But give him an extra measure of oats tonight, okay?"

"Yes, sir."

"Call me Daniel. Please?"

Luis raised one eyebrow. "Okay…Daniel."

"You *have* gone insane," Jillian persisted. "Your crazy horseback riding around the estate is just one symptom. Asking the servants to address you by your first name is another. But what I was really talking about was Jamie McNair. You had sex with her, didn't you?"

Now how the hell did she know? He'd thought Jamie's concern about the servants was unnecessary, but it appeared he was wrong. He removed Laramie's blanket and began going over his slick coat with a dandy brush.

"Whether I did or didn't, it's none of your concern, Jillian," he said sharply.

She stood staring at him, unconvinced and silently disapproving, as he worked. He grabbed a hoof pick and went to work on one muddy hoof while the horse munched some hay.

Jillian leaned her head and shoulders over the stall door. "You *did* have sex with her. God, Daniel, what were you thinking? And to shut me out as if I mean nothing to you. Who wrote to you practically every day when you were in prison? Did she?"

"Jillian. I want you to stop and listen to yourself. You are a valued and trusted employee, one I've relied on heavily for years. Relied on too much, apparently. But you're off the deep end here. I like Jamie. I like her very much, and I intend to keep seeing her. Stop acting like my mother."

"Your mother?" Jillian looked downright shocked.

Daniel had a hard time remembering that Jillian had a crush on him. He wanted to come down hard on her inappropriate behavior, but he didn't want to hurt her.

He finished off Laramie's grooming with a quick rubdown.

"Speaking of Jamie, I invited her to the party."

Jillian sighed. "Okay, Daniel. I didn't want to do this. But how much do you truly know about your new girlfriend?"

"Quite a bit, actually. I had her investigated pretty thoroughly before I decided to ask for her cooperation. I found nothing in her background to suggest she is anything but what she claims to be."

"Did you happen to look at her birth certificate?"

"Did you?" he shot back, looking at his assistant over the horse's neck. How would she get access to such a thing?

"I haven't been doing work for you and Project Justice without learning anything about investigation," she explained.

"No, I haven't seen her birth certificate. But yes, I know she was born out of wedlock. Please. Who cares? Her mother was a cleaning lady, and look how far Jamie has come."

"It's her father I'm concerned about."

Her father. Something had bothered Jamie whenever the subject of her father came up.

"What about her father?"

"His name is Chet Dotie. Ring any bells?"

Daniel dropped the cloth he was holding.

Chet Dotie. The son-of-a-bitch Harris County assistant district attorney who had prosecuted him for Andreas's murder.

Dear God. Jamie's father had sent Daniel to death row.

ON FRIDAY EVENING, Jamie stared into her closet, looking over the grim wardrobe possibilities. She had nothing appropriate for a glittery affair at Daniel's estate, and in truth she didn't feel very festive.

She'd been fired. She'd never lost a job before, and even though she'd considered the possibility ever since she first spoke to Daniel, it felt a lot worse than she'd imagined it would.

Her whole identity was wrapped up in her work as a prosecutor. Although sometimes the work was dreary, she'd always felt she was performing a necessary function in society—getting violent offenders off the street, or at least demanding a price from those who didn't follow the rules.

Without her job, who was she?

For two days she'd wandered around her apartment like a ghost, living on peanut butter and microwave popcorn, watching Oprah and Dr. Phil and Dr. Oz, all of which only served to make her feel worse.

She would have to look for another job soon. But where else could she go with her background?

She could probably get a job with a criminal-defense firm—they were always looking for former prosecutors who were ready to switch sides, since they knew the ins and outs of the system already.

But that life wasn't for her.

Depending on how this thing with Gables played out—and how vindictive Winston Chubb was—her job options could be very limited.

The same thoughts had been chasing around in her head for two days now, and she was sick of them. Maybe the party would do her good. At least the food and drink would be better than what she'd been subsisting on.

Since new clothes weren't materializing in her closet, she grabbed a plain black dress. She could jazz it up with some jewelry, her highest heels and a pair of textured stockings. If she put her hair up and wore dark lipstick, she'd pass.

As she dressed, she wondered what fantastic, stylish

creation of a dress Jillian would wear. Jamie bet it would be flashy and sexy.

It didn't matter. Jamie wasn't in competition with Jillian. As spectacular as the lovemaking between Jamie and Daniel had been, she knew it wasn't to be repeated. She didn't belong in his world and would never feel comfortable there. Daniel wasn't ready to be an equal partner to any woman. Those control issues of his weren't going to disappear overnight; he wouldn't magically be "cured" by the love of a good woman.

She was happy, though, that he thought enough of her to invite her to his party. He didn't think of her as merely a conquest or a means to an end. She genuinely believed he liked her, which had to mean she was better than the zero she'd felt like since losing her job.

When she'd finished her toilette, she inspected herself in the mirror and decided she looked pretty good. The glittering vintage rhinestones at her ears and around her neck—about the only thing of her mother's she'd kept—elevated the outfit to evening wear.

She looked somber…but elegant.

When she arrived at Daniel's estate, she got into a long queue of cars waiting to be let inside the gates. A guard was checking the credentials of each potential guest, apparently, making sure they were on the list.

This was a far cry from the parties she was used to, the kind where someone in the office shouted they were watching a game on their wide-screen TV that evening, and whoever was in earshot was welcome as long as they brought beer.

When she pulled up to the guard, he smiled. "Evening, ma'am. Can I see your invitation?"

"I didn't get one. Daniel invited me personally."

"Oh, right. You're Jamie. Sorry for the misunderstanding. You can go right in."

A valet was set up in the driveway. Jamie was happy to surrender her humble car and step into fantasyland, pretending she was someone else for a few hours.

And it was a fantasyland. Daniel's foyer—already impressive without any added effects—had been transformed into a glittering gallery of ice sculptures depicting trees and snowflakes, a full-size ice sled, a candy cane with a ribbon. Every once in a while, a handful of Hollywood-style snow would fall, sprinkling down on the guests who had paused to ooh and aah over the ice.

A uniformed man asked to take Jamie's coat, which she gladly surrendered. The wool tweed didn't go with her hastily assembled cocktail attire.

As she handed off the garment she spotted Jillian standing near the fountain—now a frozen waterfall—greeting the guests like a queen-bee hostess, just as Jamie had predicted. She wore a deep red satin dress, cut low, and a string of what were no doubt real diamonds around her long neck. Tall black heels and elbow-length gloves completed the picture.

When Jillian spotted Jamie, her smile fell away. But

then, consummate little actress that she was, she pasted on a pleasant expression. "Jamie. So glad you could make it on short notice." She took Jamie's hand in both of hers, gave it a quick squeeze, then released her and moved on to the next guest.

Poor Jillian. She probably had no idea the ax was about to fall on her world. Jamie would try to think charitably of her, now that she knew what it felt like to have the rug pulled out from under her.

Jamie followed a designated path that led into the living room. Although *living room* seemed much too tame of a term for such a huge space. The Christmas tree in here dwarfed the one in the library. It had to be twenty feet tall, lightly flocked and decorated with blue-green lights and silver balls.

She'd gotten only a swift impression of this room on earlier visits here. Now she couldn't help but admire the strange assortment of time periods that, against all logic, blended seamlessly—an Oriental rug here, a modern geometric one in complementary colors there. A chilly but sophisticated marble table was softened by a tapestry table runner and brass candlesticks; a warm sandstone fireplace was the backdrop for a modern brushed-nickel sculpture.

Daniel's interior designer must have a split personality. The final effect was impressive, but she much preferred the traditional warmth of his library.

A trio of musicians had set up in one corner, playing soft jazz. Another servant was passing around a tray of appetizers. It was Manuel, who'd brought in their snack the first night she was here.

"This one is a Grand Marnier crème puff," he was telling one of the guests. "And this, a marzipan truffle."

"I wonder how Daniel stays so trim," the woman guest enthused after taking a bite of one of the bite-size desserts. "Mmm, outstanding."

"I'll tell Chef Claude you said so."

Another server practically shoved a glass of champagne into Jamie's hand. She wasn't much of a champagne drinker, but it would at least give her something to do. She gave the golden liquid an experimental taste and was surprised at how smooth it went down. This was probably an expensive brand, something that normally wouldn't have touched her tongue.

She was so out of her element, and she didn't know anyone here except Daniel—if he was even here.

He'd said he didn't like crowds, and this definitely qualified. She wouldn't be surprised if he was hiding out somewhere—in the library or his Batcave-like basement, perhaps watching the festivities on a computer monitor. He would make a quick appearance, greet his guests and wish them a happy holiday season, then vanish like smoke.

An older woman in a floor-length blue sequined gown, her silver hair pointing every which way, was making the rounds holding a piece of mistletoe, kissing any man who would stand still long enough. Jamie suddenly recognized her and realized she did know one of the party guests.

Celeste, her forthright chauffeur.

Celeste whirled around and paused in front of Jamie. It took a moment for the light of recognition to glow from behind her thick glasses. "Jamie!"

"It's me, all right."

She handed Jamie a piece of mistletoe, then snatched it back. "Wait a minute. You don't need that. I understand you got all the kisses you can handle."

Good heavens. Just as she'd feared, she and Daniel had become the center of gossip among his employees.

"I can't imagine what you're talking about," she said primly.

A good-looking younger man—one of several Jamie had spotted among the guests—put an arm around Celeste and led her away. "Celeste, Daniel will have your hide if he finds out you're harassing an esteemed member of the district attorney's office."

Guess he hadn't gotten the memo.

"Oops," Celeste said as she allowed herself to be led away. "Forgot about that." She laughed loudly and teetered precariously on her four-inch heels.

Someone tapped Jamie on the shoulder and she turned, not knowing what to expect. But it certainly wasn't Daniel in a tuxedo that molded to his body like black paint flowing over granite—and an expression on his face like a pot about to boil over.

"Daniel." Any further words froze in her throat. He looked so good and...so angry.

"I thought about telling the front gate not to let you in. But then I realized I wanted to see you."

"What are you talking about?"

Jillian chose that moment to interrupt, bubbling over with enthusiasm. She had a tall flute full of a ruby-red liquid clasped between her hands.

"Daniel. Claude asked me to personally give this to you. It's cranberry juice and raspberry liqueur. He said you requested something without much alcohol."

"Not now, Jillian."

The dismissal caused his assistant to flinch, but she didn't give up. "He was quite insistent. You know how he can be."

Daniel seemed to be struggling to get hold of his temper. He took the flute from Jillian. "Fine, you've given it to me." He immediately set the drink down on the nearest table.

Jamie wanted to make her escape. This wasn't what she'd come here for. She'd wanted a few hours of escape and maybe, just maybe, she'd fantasized about another stolen tryst, or at least a kiss, with Daniel.

But now that he'd gone on the attack, she had to know what she'd done to infuriate him so.

Daniel gave Jillian a withering glare, and finally she got the message and skulked away.

"When did you plan to tell me that it was your father who put me in a cage for six long years?"

Oh, no. Somehow, he'd found out.

And now, *everyone* would know. Because all conversation in the room had ceased, and everyone was staring at them.

"Could…could we continue this conversation someplace more private?" she asked, mortified that he would purposely air their conflict so publicly.

"What, you don't want everyone to know that your father is the man who worked so tirelessly so that I could die? It was the case that made his whole career, you know."

"He has nothing to do with this, with *us*," she said desperately.

"Then why didn't you mention it? 'Oh, by the way, Daniel, funny coincidence. My father prosecuted your trial.' It wasn't because you had some ulterior motive, was it? Like defending dear old Dad's reputation even as you were trying to save yours?"

"Daniel, stop."

"Were you hoping I'd slip up and admit I was guilty after all? They can't re-try me for the same crime, but you could have restored the image of the man you so looked up to, the man you emulated to a T."

Jamie had no arguments left. He was right about her belief that he was guilty—at least, at first. Before she got to know him.

A handsome man with short, dark hair and a military bearing insinuated himself between her and Daniel.

"Don't you think that's enough, Daniel? Or would you like to have her publicly flogged?"

"She'll get a public flogging, all right. Just wait till the media gets hold of this story. And Jamie, you can forget about me sugarcoating your errors and omissions. You're going down."

It was too late for that. Had he not learned about her dismissal? She thought he knew everything.

The man between then deftly guided Daniel away. "Leave her be, Daniel. It's over."

Almost as if it was planned, everyone in the room looked away and went back to their hushed conversations. Even Celeste spoke in an undertone. And Jamie was left standing there like an idiot.

Her mouth was as dry as a musty old book. She grabbed the drink Daniel had abandoned and downed several swallows. But nothing—not even Claude's special drink—was going to wash away this scene from her mind. Ever.

She'd drained the glass before it registered that the stuff tasted awful. But then, she'd thought expensive Scotch was awful, too. She had no taste, apparently.

She should just leave. But instead she wandered out the back door onto the patio, where a number of heaters kept the area comfortable. The crowd parted, giving her a wide berth. Beyond the patio on the vast grounds was a snow machine creating a winter wonderland and…yes, a horse-drawn sleigh filled mostly with screaming kids.

"I'll escort you off the estate now." Jillian had appeared out of nowhere, looking as if she could hardly contain her glee.

Jamie felt the pressure building behind her eyes. She wanted to cry, but she wouldn't do it here in front of all these people. Especially not in front of Jillian. So she imagined she was one of Daniel's ice sculptures, her feelings frozen inside a block of ice.

"I'll need my coat," she said curtly.

Jillian herded her through the house and back to the foyer. "I'll get your coat. Stay right there."

Jamie felt as if she'd been flattened by a steamroller. Even if a relationship with Daniel was impossible, she hadn't wanted to lose his respect. She should have been honest with him from the very beginning. But a good lawyer didn't show all her cards until necessary.

Standing alone, forlorn, she began to shiver. Her teeth were chattering. Was it that cold? She felt light-headed, and her eyes started to swim.

She'd drunk only a half glass of champagne and those few gulps of the cranberry concoction, which was supposedly nonalcoholic. Such a small amount of alcohol wouldn't cause any noticeable impairment. Could strong emotion cause physiological symptoms?

Jillian returned and thrust Jamie's tweed coat at her. "Where's your valet ticket?"

"In m-my p-pocket, I th-think." It took her three tries to shove her arm through her coat sleeve.

Jillian put her hands on her hips. "Are you a drunk

on top of everything else?" Abruptly her combative attitude changed to one of concern. "Do I need to call you a cab?"

Jamie couldn't seem to formulate a coherent answer. The surrealistic ice sculptures began to spin around her like some crazy North Pole carousel. Then the floor tipped and the lights went out.

"DON'T YOU THINK you were a little hard on her?"

Daniel had retreated to his library, which was off-limits to the partygoers. He sat at his carved oak bar, rescued from a London pub that had been slated for destruction, nursing a Scotch that he didn't really want.

The person interrogating him was Ford Hyatt, who had followed him in here. If Ford hadn't been his most trusted investigator, he would have kicked him out.

"Her father sent me to death row."

"Her father was a prosecutor doing his job. He was set up, given phony evidence just like Jamie was."

"The man was a monster with no heart."

"So, maybe he was. Jamie had no control over what her father did."

"She should have told me. It was an important fact, given the nature of our business together. Now it will look like she had an ax to grind—that she wanted to somehow prove her father did the right thing. She's no longer impartial. We won't be able to call her to testify."

"She was never impartial. But let's just say you're

right. She did you wrong by keeping the facts of her parentage from you. Did you have to publicly humiliate her? You might have succeeded in putting her down, but your behavior didn't reflect well on you. Very few of those people in there really know you. For some of them, this is their first real contact with you. And you showed them a ranting maniac."

"I'll send out a memo, apologizing for my behavior."

Ford shook his head and poured himself some Wild Turkey.

"It's not like you. There's something going on with you and Jamie McNair besides a business relationship."

"What have you heard?"

"Nothing. But I know what I see. You wanted to hurt her, and that's not like you."

"Maybe you don't know me as well as you think. There are people out there I sincerely would like to hurt."

"But is Jamie really one of them? Or did you unload on her because you can't do anything to a man who's in his grave?"

Now that the adrenaline from his confrontation with Jamie was dissipating, Daniel could think more clearly. Maybe he'd gone overboard. He should have at least asked her why she hadn't told him about her father. And he should have talked to her in private.

He pulled a paper napkin out of his pocket and brought it to his nose. Faint traces of a lipstick scent teased him. He'd been carrying it around with him like a security blanket ever since he'd wiped Jamie's lipstick from his face the day they flew to Wichita Falls. It reminded him of everything he'd just thrown away.

"I didn't intend to do what I did," he said at last. "It's just that when I saw her, a lot of old buried feelings came surging to the surface."

He'd lost control. And he didn't like that one bit.

"Jamie gave me hope," he continued. "She made me want to rejoin the human race, to be a better person than I've been in the past. I trusted her, and you know that doesn't come easy for me."

"So you have feelings for her."

"I did. But now I see how impossible the situation is. She's a prosecutor. And it's not just her job, it's her heritage. She chose her profession because she wanted to be just like Daddy. She told me that much."

Ford shrugged and took a gulp of his drink. "You're forgetting, it's not her job anymore."

"What do you mean?" Daniel asked sharply.

"You didn't know? I thought Raleigh would have told you."

Damn. He had a message from Raleigh on his phone, but with Jillian pestering him every five minutes about some damn detail having to do with the party, he'd neglected to call her back.

"What happened?"

The phone on the bar rang, but Daniel ignored it.

"Jamie's no longer with the prosecutor's office," Ford

informed him. "She's gone, as of two days ago. Raleigh tried to call her—she had a question pertaining to the Gables case, some small thing—and she was told Jamie no longer worked there."

"And Jamie didn't let me know?" Had she been fired, or had she resigned? "If I'd known she lost her job I might not have…" Oh, who was he kidding? He hadn't planned his strategy based on anything other than raw, unfettered emotion.

It was a bad way to run his life. Everything good that had happened to him—including getting pardoned by the governor—had involved a cool head and logical, organized actions.

"I should talk to her. Apologize—at least for the way I dressed her down in a social situation."

"It's gonna have to be a mighty big apology."

Just then someone banged insistently on the door. "Daniel, are you in there?"

Jillian again. Would the woman not leave him alone?

Ford went to the door and opened it. "What is it, Jillian? This isn't a good time to disturb him."

Jillian pushed past Ford into the room. "Daniel. Jamie just collapsed in the foyer."

CHAPTER TWELVE

DANIEL'S VISION CLOSED in until all he could see was a pinprick of light. Jamie, passed out?

"I've called for an ambulance," Jillian continued, "but I thought you should know."

In a fraction of a second, Daniel's vision cleared and he was off his bar stool and striding for the door, heart pumping furiously.

His habitual mistrust forced him to ask, "Any chance she's faking?"

"I thought so at first. But when she fell she hit her head on the floor and she's bleeding everywhere. She's definitely unconscious."

A crowd of his guests had assembled in the foyer, murmuring in hushed voices. But they parted like the Red Sea as Daniel moved through them.

Jamie lay on the floor, arms and limbs at odd angles. His first thought was to go to her, draw her into his arms and breathe life and vitality into her like some mythical Prince Charming. But she was no sleeping beauty, under a magic spell, and he was sure as hell no Prince Charming.

Randall was there. Thank God. Randall had all kinds of CPR certification.

Daniel went down to one knee.

"Careful of the blood, sir," Randall said.

Daniel didn't care about any damn blood. "How is she?"

"Breathing, but unresponsive. Her pulse is slow."

Daniel lightly slapped her cheek. "Jamie, honey, wake up." If he could see some response from her, a flutter of eyelash, even, he would feel better.

He took her hand in his. "Jamie, if you can hear me, squeeze my hand."

There! He'd felt it, just the slightest tension in her fingers.

"You're going to be okay, Jamie," he said all in a rush, somehow feeling responsible for her condition. Maybe he'd only verbally assaulted her, and normally chewing someone out with words didn't produce un-consciousness, but he couldn't help feeling the two were connected.

Now her eyelashes did flutter. She could definitely hear him.

"Help's on the way. Hang in there. Please, Jamie, try to hold on, okay? I'm sorry for losing my temper with you. It was the wrong thing to do." God, he didn't want those harsh words to be the last exchange between them.

What had he been thinking? He cared about Jamie. Yes, she'd done something he didn't like, and if she were an employee he would be justified in abruptly terminating her.

But she wasn't his employee. He'd come to see her as a friend—no, clearly more than a friend, since he'd made love to her. When someone you cared about did something you didn't care for, the appropriate thing to do was talk about it, not cut them out of your life in the cruelest way possible.

The paramedics arrived. As they checked Jamie's vital signs, one of them asked questions and Jillian was there to answer them, since she was the one who'd witnessed Jamie's collapse.

"Did she have too much to drink?"

"She was only here a few minutes, and she didn't seem tipsy until right before it happened," Jillian said.

"Is she diabetic?"

"I don't know."

"She's not diabetic," Daniel supplied. "At least, I've never seen her take insulin. She hasn't mentioned any health problems."

"On any medications?"

"Not that I know of, but...truthfully, I don't know that much about her." She'd hidden her parentage from him. What else might she be hiding? She hadn't shared a lot of personal information with him.

"Has her next of kin been notified?"

"I don't think she has any family," Daniel said.

"A friend, then. Someone should go to the hospital with her."

Daniel wanted to go with her. He didn't want her to wake up alone in a strange place with no one at her side. But he didn't trust himself in that environment. What if he freaked out, like he did at the prison? That wouldn't help Jamie at all.

"Want us to go with her?" Ford asked, his fiancée, Robyn, by his side.

"Would you mind?"

"Of course we'll go," Robyn said. "I'll get our coats."

"Whatever she needs—make sure she has it," Daniel said to Ford. "I'll take financial responsibility."

"We'll make sure she gets the best of care."

"And tell her…tell her I'm sorry."

"You should tell her yourself."

"I can't go to a hospital." Too many unpleasant memories. He'd spent way too much time in hospitals after he'd gotten out of prison—first, to restore his own health. Then, watching his parents die.

"You could," Ford said. "Sometimes, Daniel, I think you use your unfortunate past as an excuse so you don't have to do anything the least bit tough or uncomfortable."

Wow. Nobody ever talked to him like that.

Ford shrugged, looking a big guilty. "There, I said it."

Daniel tried one last time to cling to his philosophy. "You don't think I've earned the right to live life on my own terms?"

"I guess if you've got the resources to do that…but you didn't corner the market on unpleasant circumstances. Raleigh witnessed her husband die in a terrible car accident. Robyn…" He lowered his voice. "Hell, Robyn lost eight years of her son's life to kidnappers. But she never felt sorry for herself."

Robyn returned with their coats. The paramedics had loaded Jamie onto a stretcher, and Daniel managed to touch her hand one last time before she was wheeled away.

Ford and Robyn followed the stretcher out the door.

He didn't feel sorry for himself, damn it. He did what he had to do, that was all.

JAMIE'S HEAD WEIGHED at least two hundred pounds, and someone was whacking at it repeatedly with a machete. Her throat felt raw, and the rest of her didn't feel much better.

Worst hangover on earth?

But she hadn't had that much to drink at Daniel's party…

Daniel. He'd found out about her father. She remembered that much, at least, and the terrible fight they'd had. But after that, events were hazy.

Had she gotten drunk? That wasn't like her. She'd never been the type to drink excessively, not even in college.

She forced her eyes open a crack, saw bright fluorescent lights, and that was when the panic hit. She wasn't at home, in her own bed.

Her eyes flew open and she gave a strange, hoarse little shriek as she tried to sit up, but a hand on her shoulder stopped her.

"Easy, it's okay, Jamie. You're safe."

Jamie's bleary eyes focused on the person leaning over her bed. A woman…

"I'm Robyn Hyatt. My husband works at Project Justice, and we were at the party."

Jamie must have looked at her blankly.

"You were at Daniel's house and you passed out suddenly. You hit your head. You were taken to Johnson-Perrone Medical Center."

"I…I don't remember." Her voice was strangely raspy. She remembered Jillian wanting to eject her from the party, and then…nothing. "Why are you here?" The question came out sounding ungrateful, so she quickly revised it. "I mean, thank you for being here… Oh. You're here to…to talk me out of suing Daniel? Don't worry, I'm not the lawsuit-happy type."

"It's not that," Robyn said emphatically. "Daniel was very worried about you. In fact, he wanted to come here himself, but…well, you know Daniel doesn't get out much."

Daniel, worried? "He didn't seem too worried about me when he chewed me out in front of a zillion people. He hates me."

"That's not true. If you could have seen him when he learned you'd fallen ill…"

"Whatever." Jamie didn't want to discuss Daniel with Robyn or anyone else. Her feelings felt as raw as her throat. "Why is my throat so sore?"

"I don't know. They won't tell me anything, since I'm not family."

Jamie opened her eyes again and looked around, taking in a few more details. "I'm in the E.R." She had an IV in one arm and various straps, patches and clamps on and around her, probably measuring her vital signs.

"Yes."

"Get me a doctor, then. Please." She didn't intend to be rude to Robyn. It was kind of her to come to the hospital and watch over her. Or maybe she was just following Daniel's orders. But this situation wasn't Robyn's fault.

"Yes, of course."

As Robyn left the cubicle, Jamie again tried to remember getting sick. But her last memory was of Jillian, announcing she would escort Jamie off the premises.

A woman in a white coat entered the cubicle. She had a round, cherubic face and a sweet smile. "Ah, you've come back to us."

"Are you my doctor?" Jamie asked, to be sure.

The woman came forward and took Jamie's hand. "I'm Dr. Novak. You gave us a scare. How do you feel?"

"On a scale of one to ten? A negative five. What happened to me?"

"You don't remember?"

"Not a thing."

"Do you remember taking any pills?"

"I don't remember what the paramedics or doctors did—"

"I mean, before you passed out."

Jamie shook her head. "No idea what you're talking about."

"Ms. McNair, you had enough barbiturates and alcohol in your blood to take down a rhinoceros."

Barbiturates?

"Secobarbital Sodium, to be exact. You might know it as Immenoctal, Novosecobarb, Seconal. Mixed with alcohol it can be deadly—"

"No. I don't take pills."

"No one is going to blame you or punish you," the doctor said gently. "You've been under a tremendous amount of stress. You lost your job, you had an argument with your boyfriend—"

Jamie jerked her hand away from the doctor's grip. "Look, let's get one thing straight. I don't know who you've been talking to, but I do not, and never have, taken any kind of tranquilizer or sleeping pills or whatever the hell you're talking about, with or without alcohol."

The doctor looked at her with cloying sympathy, and Jamie wanted to smack her.

"You think I tried to kill myself?"

"When a patient presents themselves with that amount of prescription tranqs in their blood, along with alcohol, it's usually not an accident."

"Not an accident..." Oh, God. Could someone have drugged her? Stuck her with a syringe, put the drugs in her drink? She didn't remember what happened.

At least she knew what the sore throat was about. They'd probably pumped her stomach.

"Is there someone I can call?" Dr. Novak said. "A friend, relative..."

This was a nightmare. The doctor didn't believe her. "Never mind. How soon can I get out of here?"

"I'll want to keep you overnight for observation," Dr. Novak said, now all business. "In addition to the drug overdose, you got a pretty good thump on the head. After that...we'll have to see."

Oh, good night. The doctor still didn't believe her, and Jamie was going to end up in the psych ward if she didn't do something fast.

But she couldn't think of a single person she wanted to call, someone she trusted to share this mess with, someone who would stand up and say, "Lord, no, Jamie wasn't suicidal and she most certainly would not take an overdose of tranquilizers."

Funny, Jamie hadn't really noticed the lack of close friends in her life. She had associates at her job—her former job, she amended—people she sometimes shared lunch or coffee with. She got invited to their weekend barbecues and socialized with them easily enough, talking shop, usually.

But she wasn't close to any of them. None of them had called after she'd been fired. She couldn't trust any of them, now that she was no longer one of them.

"I need to speak with a detective from the Houston police," Jamie said with as much authority as she could muster. "There's been a crime, and as we speak, someone could be destroying evidence."

"You just rest now, Jamie. I'll get the paperwork started for your admission."

Jamie spied a white garbage bag that looked as if it contained her clothes, shoes and purse. Thank God. She leaned back on her pillow and pretended to be meek and submissive. "All right. I'm resting."

Dr. Novak gave her one more worried look before leaving the room.

Once alone, Jamie sat up. She climbed down from the gurney and tested her legs. Wobbly. And she was dizzy as hell. She had to pull her IV drip bag with her, but she finally managed to reach the white garbage bag.

Settled back on the gurney, she reached inside and found the small black leather clutch she'd taken to the party. Her cell phone was inside.

"Please, dear God," she murmured, "let me get a signal in here."

Yes! She dialed the major crimes unit of the Houston P.D.

"Major Crimes, this is Sergeant Comstock."

"Abe. It's Jamie McNair."

"Jamie? I heard you got fired."

"I did, but that has nothing to do with anything right now. Someone tried to kill me, or at least make me very, very sick. I'm in the emergency room at Johnson-Perrone. Can you come? Please?"

"Did you say someone tried to kill you?"

"I was at a party. They slipped me drugs somehow."

"You mean like date rape drugs?"

"I don't know, exactly. Tranquilizers."

"I'll be there in a few minutes."

DANIEL PACED HIS DARKENED living room like a caged animal, waiting to hear from Ford. If Jamie didn't recover, he would never forgive himself. He wasn't sure how he could be responsible—he hadn't touched her—but she'd taken ill under his roof, right after he'd verbally assaulted her.

Maybe she'd eaten or drunk something she was allergic to and gone into anaphylactic shock. Maybe she'd been so upset, she'd had a stroke or a heart attack. He'd assumed she was a young, healthy woman in the prime of her life, but maybe she had some illness she hadn't mentioned.

His party guests were all gone; the festivities had broken up pretty quickly after Jamie's collapse. His ever-efficient servants had already cleaned everything up. Even the melting ice sculptures had been set outside and the paper snow put into recycling.

The place felt strangely large and empty to him, unusually quiet.

He could go to her. He could wake up Randall and have him drive...or he could drive himself, like a normal human being. But the last time he'd gone out had been such a disaster. He still tightened up inside just thinking about his visit to the prison. A hospital wouldn't be much better.

Finally the phone rang, and Daniel snatched up the receiver. "Ford?"

"Yeah. It's me. Jamie's conscious. Looks like she's gonna be okay."

Thank God. "So what happened to her?"

"You're not gonna like this."

"I already don't like it. What, for God's sake?"

"She overdosed on barbiturates and alcohol."

"She tried to...to..."

"Well, that's what everyone thought. But right now, a Houston P.D. detective is on his way over to talk to her. She claims she didn't take anything, and that someone must have slipped her the drugs somehow."

The news just got worse and worse.

"You know her better than us, Daniel," Ford said. "Did she take pills? For pain or whatever?"

"Absolutely not. Jamie wouldn't try to kill herself. That's preposterous. She was levelheaded, smart, well-grounded."

"She'd lost her job."

"She knew that was a possibility from the beginning, and it was a risk she was willing to take. She wouldn't have been happy about it, but she wouldn't be suicidal."

"Which leaves us with a pretty uncomfortable alternative. Someone at the party tried to kill her. Has she had trouble with anyone? Any conflicts with the staff?"

A painful possibility occurred to him. He hesitated to say anything; the last thing he wanted to do was falsely accuse someone. How much of a hypocrite that would make him!

"Jillian. She formed an irrational dislike for Jamie from the moment they met. But Jillian would never... I mean, I've known her since she was a kid. No way."

"There was the incident with the TV in the bathroom."

"That was an accident. A...a glue failure. Jillian couldn't be responsible for that."

"It's an awful coincidence, then. Jamie almost dying twice at your place. As a former cop, I can tell you, cops don't like coincidence."

"There's nothing I can do about that. Will you be there when Jamie talks to the detective?"

"She's asked us to be present for the interview, so we can back up her statements whenever we can."

"Try to keep a lid on things."

"I will."

"And please tell Jamie, if there's anything I can do, all she has to do is ask. She could recuperate here. I could hire a staff of twenty-four-hour nurses, her own private doctor, whatever she needs."

"I'll tell her. But Daniel, don't hold your breath. You weren't exactly the most gracious host last time she was there. And considering she almost got killed at your place twice, she won't be too anxious to spend time under your roof."

All of which meant, if he wanted to see her and repair the damage he'd done, he was going to have to go to her.

Maybe he could. For Jamie, maybe he could do the impossible.

Tomorrow. Would tomorrow be too late?

"JAMIE, HAVE ANY OTHER attempts been made to harm you?" Lieutenant Abe Comstock asked. He was a handsome man with dark skin and the beginnings of gray at his temples. At this hour of the night, his shirt, which stretched over wide shoulders and muscular arms, was wrinkled and his tie askew.

Jamie liked Abe. He was smart and no-nonsense, and she was glad to be able to tell her story to someone who knew she wasn't a crackpot—*if* the D.A.'s office hadn't poisoned his mind against her already.

She'd asked Robyn and Ford Hyatt to stay with her during the interview. They were all crammed into

Jamie's hospital room—she'd finally been admitted sometime around 2:00 a.m.

She started to say no, that no one had tried to harm her before the previous evening. But then she remembered the TV incident. "When I was staying at Daniel's, I was about to take a bath when a TV fell off the wall where it was mounted, into the tub. I could have been electrocuted. I thought it was just a freak accident."

"It was an accident," Ford put in. "The company that put the TV in admitted it was their fault. Something about the wrong kind of glue."

Abe looked at Ford. "And you know this…how?"

"Daniel told me."

Abe made a few scratches in his notebook, then returned his attention to Jamie. "You say you and Daniel had a very public argument a few minutes prior to your getting sick. What did you argue about?"

Jamie saw no way out of this. "He'd just found out the prosecutor who sent him to death row was my father."

Abe's eyes widened and Robyn gasped, but Ford obviously already knew.

"I should have told him, and he had a right to be angry," Jamie said.

"Do you think he was angry enough to harm you?"

"He was very angry," Jamie said. "But honestly? He would never hurt me physically. I just can't see it."

"Who else would want you dead?" Abe asked. "Because without another viable suspect, Daniel Logan is looking very suspicious."

This wasn't the direction she wanted Abe to go in. "There's something else. I've been working to prove that a man I prosecuted is actually innocent," Jamie said. "We now have the DNA of an alternate suspect. Maybe…"

"Project Justice does make plenty of people angry," Ford said. "When someone is falsely convicted, the real perpetrator gets away with his crime. Then we come along with new evidence, and the perp gets nervous. Just a few months ago, my wife was assaulted by one such person."

"And then there was Raleigh," Robyn said. "Our chief legal counsel almost got pushed off a rooftop—"

"That one, I remember," Abe said. "And I thought my work was dangerous. But how would this as-yet-unnamed murderer be at Daniel's office party? Doesn't make sense."

Jamie sagged in defeat.

"There is one other possibility we haven't mentioned," Ford said, sounding supremely uncomfortable. "One other person at the party who doesn't like you, Jamie."

Jamie looked at him questioningly. "I don't think— Oh."

"Who?" Abe prodded.

Jamie sighed. "Jillian, Daniel's assistant. She was jealous of me. Mistakenly," Jamie added quickly, hoping it didn't come to light that she and Daniel had had sex. "She's rather territorial about Daniel, and I think she saw me as an invader—coming into his home, spending time with him, sharing meals with him. We were working very closely on this case and she resented me."

"Everybody knows Jillian has a...a thing for her boss," Ford added.

"Jillian wouldn't hurt anyone," Robyn argued.

"She might not have intended to kill anybody," Ford said. "Maybe she just wanted Jamie to act drunk...make a fool of herself."

Abe made more notes. "I've always wanted to see Daniel Logan's house. Now, I guess I have a reason to drop by."

"Jillian has the guest list, too," Jamie said, feeling the first stirrings of unease about bringing this mess down on Daniel. If only this was some huge mistake. But blood tests don't lie, and she *was* drugged. And it *did* happen at the party, there was no question.

Abe finally left. He didn't offer her any protection, citing budget cuts and a lack of evidence suggesting she was in urgent mortal danger.

She didn't argue with him. She was too exhausted.

"I'll keep an eye on things," Ford offered. "Daniel would want that. He's offered to let you recuperate in his home. He said he would hire a staff of private nurses to watch over you every minute."

"No."

"I told him you probably wouldn't be too keen on the idea. But he feels bad, Jamie."

If he felt all that bad, wouldn't he be here? If he cared

about her at all… But instead he'd sent his soldiers, two of the hundreds of people who went out into the world to live his life for him.

"Some things his money can't fix," she said to no one in particular, "no matter how many nurses he can hire."

Robyn looked as if she wanted to argue, but she kept quiet.

"I appreciate everything you two have done for me tonight. Really. But tomorrow I'll get out of this place. I just need to go home and forget tonight ever happened."

"Good luck with that," Ford said. "If someone truly tried to kill you, the ordeal is just beginning."

CHAPTER THIRTEEN

DANIEL HAD MANAGED TO CATCH a couple of hours' sleep. But by the time he received word that the police had arrived, he was awake, showered, shaved and dressed. He'd checked in with Ford; Jamie was safe and sleeping normally. He'd sent Randall to relieve Ford and Robyn, who were probably beyond exhausted by now.

He met Lieutenant Abe Comstock in the foyer and showed him into the library.

"You had a party here last night?" Comstock began conversationally, looking around with obvious curiosity.

"Yes, that's right."

It had been a long time since Daniel had last been interrogated, but he knew the routine. Abe would act like a pal, try to get him to relax, ease into the subject gradually. But Daniel already knew he would be considered a suspect. He had argued with Jamie, loudly and publicly, just minutes before her collapse.

He had a motive—revenge. He couldn't kill the man who had wrongly prosecuted him, but he could kill that man's daughter. That was exactly what Abe Comstock must be thinking right now.

"Place sure is clean."

"My staff is very efficient."

"Do you always clean this thoroughly right after a party? 'Cause it always takes me and the missus days to find all the half-empty beer cans."

"This is the first party I've had in this house since my parents died. Please, sit down."

Comstock parked himself in a red leather armchair, and Daniel sat on the leather sofa—the one he and Jamie had made love on. He probably should have chosen a different locale, one that wouldn't remind him of her— and what he'd lost—in such a visceral way.

Daniel decided to go on the offensive. "I've already spoken with Ford Hyatt this morning. He says I'm suspect number one in the attempted murder of Jamie McNair."

"You don't seem too surprised."

"I was plenty surprised—and horrified—when I learned Jamie had been drugged. I also understand exactly why you think I did it. I'm willing to cooperate in every way possible so that you can find out who's responsible. You can search anywhere on the estate. I'll give you a complete list of everyone who was here.

"I'll do anything in my power to make you see that I would never hurt Jamie."

"Are you involved with her?"

"Yes." It was true, and if there was one thing his work with Project Justice had taught him, it was that you never lied during an interrogation, even if your answer seemingly had nothing to do with the crime. It would come back to bite you.

"I felt betrayed when I found out she hadn't been completely truthful with me. I did lose my temper. I said some things intended to be hurtful. But that was as far as it went."

Comstock asked a lot more questions; he wanted a minute-by-minute timeline of Daniel's whereabouts. He had Daniel walk him through the various locations involved.

Then he asked to see Jillian.

"She didn't do it," Daniel said. "From the beginning she didn't like or trust Jamie. But she was the one who found out about Jamie's father and told me. That was her revenge. She wanted me to cut Jamie out of my life, and I did. She wouldn't have any reason to act."

"Unless she knew you and Jamie had…"

"I don't think she knew."

"Women always know. They just do." It sounded like Comstock knew from personal experience.

"I'll call Jillian."

But before he could, Jillian walked into the room. Maybe she'd been eavesdropping. Wearing a pair of wrinkled jeans and a plain blue T-shirt, she didn't look quite as well put together as usual. Her hair looked as if she'd just gotten out of bed, and she wore no makeup.

She'd probably been up late last night, he reasoned, seeing to the cleanup.

"I was just getting ready to call you," Daniel said.

"This is Lieutenant— Jillian, what's wrong?" Her eyes were filled with tears, and his first thought was that she'd heard something from the hospital and Jamie had taken a turn for the worse. "Is it Jamie?"

"It's Chef Claude. He was in a car accident this morning, on his way to work. His mother just called. He's got a broken leg, a bruised kidney…and he's…he's lost an eye."

"Oh, dear God. Is he going to live?"

"She said yes. But she doesn't know if he'll ever be able to work again."

"Of course he will. We'll get him the best doctors, the best physical therapists. Call his mother back. Tell her we'll spare no expense."

"This Claude is your employee?" Comstock asked.

"He's much more than that," Daniel replied, wanting to crawl into a hole and forget the last twenty-four hours had ever happened. "I've known him since he was a kid. He was an assistant in the kitchen when I was growing up. While I was away at college, my dad sent Claude to the Cordon Bleu school in Paris. He was my first business partner."

"I didn't know that," Jillian said.

"We opened a restaurant. It's not something I mention much, seeing as it was a crashing failure."

"You had a business failure?" Comstock asked, seemingly fascinated. "Was the food that bad?"

"Claude's cooking wasn't the problem. His ambition was. He wanted to expand too much, too fast, when we didn't have enough cash flow. We went our separate ways after that. But when I got out of prison, my father tracked him down and hired him to work here—for me. He's been here ever since."

"Who should I put in charge of the kitchen?" Jillian asked.

"Cora. But wait a minute," Daniel said. "Lieutenant Comstock wants to talk to you."

"Me?"

"Someone tried to kill Jamie McNair," Daniel said.

Jillian took a step backward and blinked. "You think I had something to do with it?" she shrieked.

"Jillian. Calm down. Just answer Lieutenant Comstock's questions. I urge you to answer truthfully."

"What do you want to know?"

"You were there when Jamie and your employer argued," Comstock said. "I want to know what you saw, what you heard. For instance, was she eating or drinking anything at the time?"

"She was poisoned?"

Comstock said nothing, just waited for her to answer the question.

"Oh, my God." Jillian turned the color of grits. She grabbed on to the nearest table as she swayed on her feet, then sank onto a footstool. "Daniel, do you remember why I interrupted you and Jamie?"

"Frankly, no. Your timing was very bad, and I was focused on Jamie."

"I was trying to give you a drink. Claude made it special. For you."

Daniel strained his brain. "I do remember something…about cranberries?"

"Yes. You took the drink from me, but you didn't taste it. You set it aside."

"Yeah…"

"After you walked away from Jamie, she picked up that drink and chugged down the whole thing. Oh, my God. I'm the one who poisoned her."

"Wait. So you were trying to poison *me?*"

Her eyes widened in horror. "Oh, Daniel, of course not. I would never hurt you. I lo—" She caught herself. "I think you're a wonderful person."

Comstock hadn't missed the slip.

"But if that drink was poisoned…" Comstock's voice trailed off.

"Claude gave it to me. To give to Daniel. Jamie wasn't the target. You were."

"RED ROSES, HUH?" Robyn plucked the card from the bouquet sitting on a shelf near Jamie's hospital bed. Jamie already knew what was written on the card by heart: *Dearest Jamie, please be well soon. Daniel.* When Robyn read it she looked at Jamie with a speculative gleam in her eye.

"He's been very kind," Jamie said.

Jamie spent two days in the hospital. Since Daniel had told them to spare no expense, he would pay for everything, they'd run every test imaginable on her. They'd tested her kidneys and liver, they'd looked at her stomach lining, they'd done an MRI on her head because of the concussion.

She'd been moved to a larger room, and instead of hospital food, she'd been offered meal choices from nearby restaurants. She'd also had fresh flowers delivered to her room both days. Her TV had offered all the premium channels.

She'd had no idea a hospital would have VIP suites.

She'd even agreed to a psych evaluation—just to put to rest any lingering suspicion that she might have tried to kill herself.

At first, she'd been irritated by Daniel's high-handed ways. Didn't he get the message? She wasn't impressed by his money and power. Other women might swoon over the fact that he could get the chef at the hottest restaurant in town to personally prepare chicken Kiev for her.

But that wasn't what she wanted from Daniel.

She wanted him. All of him. Not just the parts that were convenient for him to show her. She wanted him to get out into the world and live. She wanted him to admit he needed help, and get it.

She wanted him to let go of the past, because until he did, he couldn't move forward toward the future—with her.

But as it stood, he was just another project like all those men her mother tried to fix. Granted, he was a rich, handsome, charismatic project. But she'd made the mistake of falling in love with his potential—the well-adjusted Daniel Logan who didn't exist and probably never would.

"Red roses don't say 'kind,'" Robyn said. "Men don't send red roses to associates or friends or relatives."

"He probably didn't even pick them out."

"Well, it wasn't Jillian. She'd have sent you dead flowers."

At the mention of Jillian's name, Jamie sobered. "They haven't arrested anyone, have they?"

"Not that I've heard."

Jamie hadn't heard any updates on the investigation, either, but that wasn't surprising. Often the crime victim was the last one to know.

Dr. Novak paid Jamie one last visit before she was discharged. "I see you have someone here to drive you home."

"Yes." Robyn and Ford had offered to let Jamie stay at their house for a few days, and she had reluctantly agreed that it might not be a good idea to stay alone.

"Have they caught the person who drugged you?" the doctor asked.

"Not that I know of."

Dr. Novak lowered her voice. "So what's it like, having a boyfriend who could buy a foreign country, if he wanted to?"

Jamie laughed. "He's not my boyfriend."

"Honey, a man doesn't send flowers like that—" she

pointed to a vase containing two dozen red roses "—to a friend."

"What did I tell you?" Robyn said.

"Daniel doesn't do anything small, that's all."

But maybe the roses did mean something, if two people had pointed out the significance in the span of five minutes.

Jamie signed a seemingly endless stack of paperwork. Then finally she was rolled downstairs in a wheelchair to the front door.

Robyn led her to a gorgeous silver Jaguar parked at the curb. Either teachers were getting paid more than they used to, or ex-cops turned investigators for Project Justice earned a darn good living.

Jamie stuffed her cute rolling train case—courtesy of Daniel—and the flowers into the backseat. She jumped when a golden retriever occupying the far seat leaned over to sniff the flowers.

Oh, no. Someone was already behind the wheel, and it wasn't Robyn.

"Daniel." Her heart began a staccato rhythm behind her ribs and her stomach fluttered madly. No wonder Robyn had insisted she put on lipstick and comb her hair before leaving the hospital.

Seeing no way out of this, she climbed into the passenger seat, sending Robyn a withering look.

"Bye-bye, now," Robyn said as she closed the car door and sauntered away.

Jamie felt the urge to leap out of the car and flee

to the safety of the hospital. She wasn't ready to face Daniel. He'd been so angry with her during their last face-to-face conversation, and...

"Daniel," she said again, blinking stupidly at him. "You're driving a car."

"Did you think I couldn't drive?"

"I thought you preferred limousines with bulletproof glass, and drivers and bodyguards." She still wondered if she was dreaming. She'd longed for Daniel to show her that he cared. She'd wanted him to come to her. And he'd done it—though not without a manipulative twist in the mix.

"So, this is something new for me," he said casually.

"How do you like it so far?"

"Well, I haven't turned into a pumpkin yet. I imagined this horde of reporters following me wherever I went, like they did after I got out of prison. But you know what? No one's interested. They've moved on."

"Don't underestimate the media. It's possible they simply haven't noticed you yet." And when news got out about an attempted murder at his mansion, interest would be revived.

So far, though, the press hadn't caught on.

"How are you, Jamie?" he asked. "You look much better than you did last time I saw you."

"I would have to. I was unconscious and bleeding last time you saw me."

"Are you okay? I had no trouble providing you with

roses and four-star meals, but the one thing I couldn't buy was information about your health. Hospitals take privacy very seriously."

"I'm fine. The doctor said no lasting damage from the tranquilizers."

He expelled a breath he'd been holding. "Thank God. I was so worried about you."

"Um, maybe we should go." A couple of people had stopped on the sidewalk to gawk at the gorgeous, expensive car. And though the tinted windows prevented them from seeing inside, they were curious.

"Right. Away we go." He put the car in gear and smoothly pulled away from the curb, then accelerated toward the hospital exit.

Daniel couldn't believe he was actually out driving a car with a beautiful woman beside him. Inside, he was a lot shakier than he let on. But it was thrilling, too. All this time he'd imagined he was in complete control of his life, when in reality he'd been turning over control to everybody else—Jillian, Randall, even Claude.

Claude. Thinking about his old friend made his heart constrict.

"You're taking me to the Hyatts' house, right?" Jamie asked.

"I thought we'd go for a drive. If you're not too tired."

"I'm exhausted. You'd think lying around for two days, I'd be raring to go. But getting poked and prodded nonstop—thanks for that, by the way—wore me out. Couldn't sleep, either."

"A hospital isn't like staying in the penthouse at the St. Regis," Daniel said. "But I'm sure Ford and Robyn have a nice, quiet guest room." He sounded disappointed.

"We don't have to go straight there," Jamie said suddenly. "It's actually nice, sitting in this comfy leather seat, watching the world go by."

The weather was perfect—sunny and in the sixties. Hot, muggy Houston summers might not be the envy of everyone in the world, but the balmy winters made up for it.

"Do you even have a driver's license?" Jamie asked.

"I've kept it current, even though I wasn't actually driving."

"Did the DMV come to you?"

He grinned but didn't answer, because she was absolutely right. He couldn't remember the last time he stood in line anywhere.

He merged onto the freeway, amazed at how quickly the skills required for driving in the kamikaze Houston traffic came back to him. Maybe his grip on the steering wheel was a bit tight, but that was more due to his nearness to Jamie than the cars swerving lane to lane all around him.

Jamie was being civil, but that didn't mean she'd forgiven him. Or forgotten. He could never take those harsh words back.

"Have the police reached any conclusions?" she asked.

"They haven't told you anything?"

"Not a word. It's awful, being out of the loop."

"Actually, there is a suspect."

"Is it Jillian? Daniel, I did give the police her name. But I told them in no uncertain terms I didn't believe she would stoop that low."

"It's not Jillian, although they're still looking at her. It's someone we never considered, and frankly, I'm a bit skeptical. Are you hungry?"

"Starving, but don't leave me in suspense like that. Who?"

"Claude. My chef."

Daniel's revelation was met with thundering silence.

He didn't rush to explain. He wanted to hear her take on it, without any preconceived notions. So while he let her absorb what he'd just said, he got off the freeway and, prompted by his GPS, drove to a little-known urban park, a small slice of green grass and ancient live oak trees that had been spared the bulldozer for over a hundred years.

"Why are we stopping?" Jamie asked as Daniel pulled up to a parking meter, then realized he didn't have change. Such an ordinary thing, pocket change. Everybody had it but him.

"Picnic."

"Are you kidding?"

"No. I packed the basket myself. It's not as fancy as Claude would have made, but you'll like it."

"Claude. Are you going to tell me why you think he tried to kill me? 'Cause I don't have a clue."

"I will. If you'll loan me all the quarters in your purse. I'll pay you back with interest."

Jamie laughed. God, it was good to hear her laugh. "There's something ironic about the unemployed government employee loaning the billionaire a few quarters."

"I'm not a billionaire, you know. After the last stock-market crash, it's down to only about seven hundred million."

"The funny thing is, I think you're serious." She grabbed the small bag he'd had sent to the hospital, along with a change of clothes he'd retrieved from one of the guest-room closets and a few toiletries. Inside she found her small, black clutch purse, the one she'd brought to his party, and fished around.

"You're in luck. Three quarters."

"Perfect."

"Why don't you just risk the ticket? It's not like thirty-five bucks is going to bankrupt you."

"True. But that was the old Daniel, the one who thought he didn't have to follow the rules of ordinary people. I've changed, Jamie. Or at least, I'm trying to change. You've made me see my life for what it was, and I didn't care for it too much."

He got out, tipped his seat forward, snapped a leash on Tucker's collar. The dog clamored out of the backseat.

Daniel stuffed the borrowed quarters into the meter as Jamie climbed out, looking around curiously.

Daniel pressed a button on his keychain and the trunk popped open. He grabbed a basket and an old quilt from the trunk.

"You're serious? We're going on a picnic?"

"You don't want to?"

"I'm too hungry to turn down food."

They set out to walk the two blocks to the park.

His park.

It was a little triangle of green space at a nondescript intersection in a not-so-great part of downtown. But despite the blowing trash and graffiti that marred the blocks on all sides, this park was pristine. It was surrounded by a wrought-iron fence, but the gate was always open.

A sign over the gate proclaimed the park's name.

"Logan Park," Jamie read. "Coincidence? I think not."

"See that building right there?" He pointed to an old redbrick office building. "That was the first location of Logan Oil. My grandfather gave this land to the city, with the provision that it always be kept a public park. He set up a trust for the perpetual care of the land and improvements."

"He was ahead of his time, your grandfather." She stepped through the gate. "It's beautiful. I've worked downtown my whole adult life and I never knew this was here."

"Most people don't."

They had their choice of picnic spots—a couple of old stone tables and benches, a stucco pavilion with a red tiled roof made to look like an old Spanish mission or a sunny spot on a patch of soft green grass.

"Do you mind sitting on the ground?"

"No, I don't mind."

Daniel let Tucker off the leash, since no one else was around. The retriever set about sniffing every tree, bush and bench, probably happy for a new space to explore where other dogs had been.

Jamie helped Daniel spread out the old quilt. They sat down on it and Daniel opened the basket. He plucked out a block of cheddar cheese, already cut into slices, some crackers, sliced apples and green grapes, and two bottles of mineral water.

"I was expecting some gourmet concoction," Jamie said. "But I love crackers and cheese."

"The police confiscated almost everything from my kitchen. This was about all that was left."

"Claude," she said, as if suddenly remembering. "Tell me again why you think he tried to kill me. His name certainly never came up in the Christopher Gables investigation."

Tucker, apparently satisfied that the park was free of marauding squirrels and enemy dogs, flopped down on the grass near the quilt with a contented sigh.

Daniel scratched the dog's belly. "Not you. Me. You

just got in the way. Do you remember the drink Jillian tried to give me when we were arguing?"

Jamie tried. She had a vague memory of something red, but that was it. She shook her head.

"You drank it. The whole thing, according to several witnesses. A few minutes later you passed out suddenly. You'd drunk some champagne earlier, which only magnified the effects of the tranquilizer."

"I do remember the champagne. Oh, Daniel, why would Claude want to kill you? That doesn't make sense, either."

"I didn't think so. But Claude was supposedly in a car accident early on the morning after the party. Now, he can't be found. The police are looking for him."

"It does seem suspicious that he would disappear," Jamie agreed.

What no one else knew was that his own people were investigating Claude, too. In addition to trying to determine his whereabouts, they were searching for any possible connection Claude had to either of the two murders.

"We have only Jillian's word that Claude gave her the tainted drink that was meant for me," Daniel said.

"So it could have been Jillian herself who doctored the drink."

"It's another scenario the police are considering. Frankly, I don't like either one. All those years I insulated myself from the outside world, surrounding myself with only the most trusted people, thinking I was safe. To discover a lethal threat coming from my inner circle—it's life-changing."

Jamie said nothing. She threw a grape to Tucker, who snapped it up in midair.

"I'd like to apologize for the way I treated you at the party. It was horrible. I was horrible."

A shadow crossed her face. "It certainly took me off guard. Not the Daniel I thought I knew."

"That angry man isn't someone I often show the world. But he's there, inside me. The fact I was so out of control—that was another revelation for me. Again, I thought I had control of my life. But not everything. Can you ever find it in your heart to forgive me?"

She gave him a wry smile. "Can you ever forgive me for not telling you who my father was? I meant to. I planned to. But it never seemed the right time.

"At first, it didn't matter. I assumed my association with you would be brief. By the time I realized you'd become—" she stopped and took a sip of mineral water "—more than a friend to me, it was too late to tell you without some fallout. So I took the easy way out, and didn't say anything. I didn't think you'd find out until I was ready. Who told you?"

"Jillian, at her most scarily efficient. She knows more about investigating than I thought. She got hold of your birth certificate."

"I'm sure she enjoyed telling you all about it."

"She thought she was protecting me. I spoke to her this morning. I told her things were going to change, and that there would always be a place for her on my staff—but not as my assistant."

"Ouch. How'd that go?"

"Not well, but it needed to be said."

"You've really put yourself outside your comfort zone today, Daniel. I'm amazed."

"And impressed?" he asked.

"Daniel, you don't have to impress me. You just have to be yourself. You once told me you were broken, but I don't believe that. Not anymore. You've showed me today that you're capable of change. You see yourself clearly, and you're willing to fix the things in your life that aren't working. That's extraordinarily healthy."

"So you are impressed?" he asked with a grin.

"Yes. Clearly you have more work ahead of you," she teased. "But I am impressed."

"A lot of things in my life weren't working. For instance, I wasn't the kind of man you could fall in love with. Could that change?"

She reached up and touched his face. "Yes, Daniel, it could." She raised up on her knees, leaned in and touched her lips to his.

It was the sweetest kiss Daniel had ever experienced, filled with so much promise it took his breath away.

He reached for her, but she pulled away and sat back down on the quilt, looking guilty. "Probably not the best decision I ever made."

"Why not? I can't think of a better occasion than a picnic for two people to make out."

"I don't want to rush things, Daniel. With all that's going on, I have so much to think about."

"Nothing's ever perfect. When I was in prison, I spent a lot of time regretting the things I didn't do, the chances I didn't take."

"The women you didn't bed."

"That, too," he admitted.

"You aren't going to prison again," Jamie stated emphatically. "Not unless the police think that you mixed the drink Jillian gave you, intending to murder yourself."

"The police have come to stupider conclusions." Daniel pushed himself to his feet, then offered Jamie his hand. "Come with me. I want to show you something."

She willingly placed her hand in his and pulled herself up. He was amazed she trusted him so easily. The Jamie he'd first met two weeks ago trusted no one.

He led her to the pavilion, then to the wooden slat door that was part of the miniature mission-style building. Grateful that he'd thought to bring the key, he opened it.

It was just a large storage room where the man who took care of the park left his lawn equipment and paint. Everything was clean and well cared for, and the room smelled faintly of earth and freshly mown grass.

"What's in here?"

Daniel closed the door behind them.

"You, me and some privacy."

She laughed nervously. "You're kidding, right?"

He took her hand and guided it toward his zipper. He wanted her to feel just exactly how serious he was. "I've said in so many words how sorry I am for heaping blame on you where it wasn't warranted, for making you the scapegoat for anger that had nowhere else to go. But words don't really cut it, do they? Let me show you, Jamie."

"You want to have sex in a garden shed?"

CHAPTER FOURTEEN

DANIEL PUSHED JAMIE up against the wall and kissed her, hard. "You mean the smell of fertilizer doesn't turn you on?" he murmured in her ear.

"I don't smell fertilizer." Her voice was hoarse with need, and her eyes had gone all smoky. "I smell fertile earth and grass and…machine oil." And never had there been a more potent aphrodisiac.

"You can say no. You did just get out of the hospital."

She didn't answer with words. Instead, she peeled her thin cashmere sweater over her head and tossed it aside, allowing him to admire her in a wispy, barely-there bra.

Amazing what a tiny scrap of lace could do to a man's brain, sending hormones and neurotransmitters racing all over his body, hooking up with receptors everywhere in an instant, causing his erection to surge forward, begging for freedom.

The delicate skin of her breasts blushed pink as he gazed at them.

"Your first time out of the house on your own in months—"

"Years," he corrected her.

"—and you go completely berserk."

He got busy unbuttoning his shirt, pulling it out from his jeans. "The freedom has gone to my head."

"I'd say it's gone somewhere else in your body." She unfastened his jeans and pulled them down, along with his boxers. His erection sprang forward, and she immediately leaned over and took him into her mouth.

She'd done the same thing the last time they'd had sex. She must like it, he thought hazily. It was a good quality in a woman. But he wanted to be inside her.

It took a monumental amount of willpower, but he put his hands on her shoulders and pushed her away. "Too much."

"No, it's not. It's just enough." She drew him inside her mouth again, and again he pulled away. "I want to make love to you, Jamie."

"I'm not sure that's possible in here."

"Of course it is." *Where there's a will, there's a way.* He spied a stack of bagged garden soil, stacked four deep and two wide, that would make a dandy bed.

She saw it too and shook her head. "I'm not having sex on a pile of manure."

"It's not manure. It's good clean dirt in nice plastic bags."

"Works for me." She kicked off her loafers and shucked her jeans. They piled their clothes on the plastic bags and fell onto the impromptu bed, both of them naked and hungry.

He spotted the bruise on the inside of her elbow, where her IV had been, which prompted a stab of guilt. "I shouldn't be ravishing a woman who just got out of the hospital."

She wrapped her arms around his neck and pulled him on top of her. "You are the only medicine I need, Daniel Logan." She kissed him as if she meant business, and he forgot everything except how much he wanted to be inside her. He wanted them to be one. He was crazy about her. Somehow, she'd brought him back to life when he didn't even realize he'd been numb, almost dead, inside.

His awakening was both painful and thrilling.

He ran his hands lightly up and down her body as if he'd never felt a woman's body before. Everything felt new, fresh, exciting—her hip bone under his thumb, the soft swell of her breasts. He kissed the inside of her elbow where the bruise was, then her wrists. He placed his mouth over one nipple and sucked gently, and she whimpered and wiggled in response.

"Daniel." Her name on his lips was a caress, stoking his desire more fiercely than any stroke of her hands or her mouth could. She was so alive, so vital, and yet he knew now that he could lose her with careless words and actions.

The first time he'd made love to her was mind-blowing, but now it meant so much more.

"Daniel," she said, more insistently this time.

"Are you sure you're ready?" He reached between

their bodies and touched her soft mound. His fingers sought the warmth between her legs. She was slick and hot, but suddenly she clamped her legs closed.

"Stop being so freaking concerned about me. You, inside me. Now."

No one ever dared speak to him like that. It was a turn-on.

"Yes, ma'am."

She opened her legs again and he poised himself above her. She wrapped her hand around him and guided him inside her. The outside world slipped away. The universe contracted until all that was left were Jamie and himself, joined as one, soaring together. Each stroke brought him closer to paradise as she alternately encouraged him and cursed him for prolonging her climax.

It wasn't deliberate. But the fates intervened so that when he finally reached that peak from which he could not return, she did, too. Their cries mingled as he released himself into her, waves of ecstasy washing over them in violent crescendos that gradually calmed to ripples in a pond. Their surroundings came back, and Jamie gave one last shiver.

"Well," she said.

"Exactly." He laughed in pure delight. "I think I'm going to like rejoining the human race."

Just then, Tucker started barking.

"Oh, hell, someone's out there," Daniel said, reluctantly separating himself from Jamie.

"Great, just great!" She moved faster than he'd ever

seen her move, grabbing her clothes and wiggling into them in a fast-forward, reverse striptease that he cataloged in his memory for review later.

"The door's locked," he reminded her.

"Don't other people have keys? Like the gardener?"

Tucker's barking grew more frenzied just as the knob turned. Daniel thrust Jamie behind him, ready to face the intruder.

But the middle-aged man who entered hardly looked threatening in his overalls and worn denim jacket. In fact, he was the one who looked surprised and a little scared when he spotted them.

He unleashed a stream of frantic Spanish. To his surprise, Jamie replied—in what sounded like pretty competent Spanish to him—while nudging Daniel toward the door. The man stood aside and allowed them to make their escape.

Tucker greeted Daniel enthusiastically, tail wagging, and Daniel gave him a quick scratch behind the ears without pausing. "Good boy. Thanks for the warning." The dog would never bite anyone, but Daniel was grateful the gardener hadn't hurt his dog or called animal control.

He and Jamie quickly packed up the picnic and made a hasty exit from Logan Park.

"What did you say to him?" Daniel asked.

"Just that we meant him no harm and we were leaving. He thought we were trespassers."

"He didn't recognize me?"

"Apparently not."

"Good." Daniel laughed as he started the car. He was about to pull away from the curb when his phone rang.

Ordinarily he would have let it go to voice mail: bad manners to take phone calls when he was entertaining a lady. But given that he was expecting all kinds of urgent news, he felt compelled to answer.

"Go ahead," Jamie said.

Daniel checked the caller ID. The call came from Project Justice. "Daniel Logan."

"Daniel. It's Mitch. I hope you're sitting down."

"Spill it."

"I've been doing deep background on Claude Morel. At first, he didn't appear to be connected to the Frank Sissom murder. But it turns out that while you were in prison, he was in business with…wait for it… Christopher Gables."

"Are you kidding me?" Daniel's mind struggled back into its habitual pathways, analyzing data, finding the patterns. But this one wasn't difficult. In each murder case, Claude had been the former business partner of the man accused of the crime.

"They opened a French restaurant about ten years ago. The business filed for bankruptcy after only nine months."

"Then it's him. That's the connection we've been missing."

"Theoretically, he might have tried to kill you—or at least put you out of commission and buy himself some time—because you were getting too close to the truth."

"We have his DNA. He must have known that."

"I have more. Flight reservations for two, in the names of Claude Morel and Marie Morel, departing Houston Intercontinental at 4:17 p.m. this afternoon headed for Paris. Marie is his mother, right?"

"Yes." And a sweet little lady, at least in his memory. "Call Abe Comstock at the Houston P.D. Fill him in. If Claude boards that plane we've lost him, and probably any chance for a DNA match."

"Is there time?" Mitch asked.

"We have to try. Without knowing his current location—"

"Wait, I have an address. From Marie's credit card."

"Give it to me."

"Seventeen-oh-three Templeton."

Daniel punched the address into his onboard GPS. It took him a couple of tries to get the unfamiliar gadget to respond, but finally he had a map.

"I'm about nine miles away. I can go there and…" And what? "See if he's there."

"Will you…send Randall?"

"I'm in my car. I can drive there."

"Wait, you're…*where?*"

Daniel didn't have time to explain his sudden metamorphosis from recluse to man-about-town. "Send Randall as backup. Call him after you call the police. Quickly."

Daniel disconnected, set the phone on the console and pulled out into the street, very nearly colliding with a Toyota approaching from behind.

"Watch out!" Jamie yelled, but Daniel had already put on the brakes, and the car swerved around them.

"Sorry."

"What's going on?" she asked urgently.

"Claude murdered both Andreas and Frank Sissom, that's what. Mitch found the link." He pulled into traffic, then cut across to the left turn lane.

"Where? How?" She knew the name of every person connected to Sissom. She'd been studying this case for weeks.

"Claude and Christopher once owned a restaurant together. But he knows we're on to him—that's why he tried to kill me. He's trying to leave the country and I'm not about to let that happen."

"So, call the police!"

"Mitch is handling that. But convincing takes time. Comstock might not be available. He might be off duty. Mitch will have to explain how he got the information he has, which could be dicey."

"He got it by hacking?"

"I don't ask how Mitch gets his information. We can't wait for all this to filter through the proper channels. Claude is probably packing as we speak. He might already be on his way to the airport."

She looked at the GPS screen, then back at Daniel as he pulled a U-turn. "Wait—we're going to Claude's house?"

"His mother's house, I think. Claude lives in Montrose."

"But if you're right, he's a cold-blooded murderer! What are we going to do? We're not cops, we don't have guns or badges or any kind of authority."

"You're right. I wasn't planning to confront him, but it could be dangerous. I'll drop you off someplace safe on the way."

"You will not. Daniel, *I'll* call Comstock. He'll listen to me." Maybe. She dug into her purse for her cell phone. But after two days in the hospital without a charge, it was dead.

"Mitch is already doing that. Anyway, Comstock would just tell us to go home and lock the door."

Which would be very good advice. Just exactly when had Daniel gone from agoraphobic to action hero?

"Hang tight, Jamie. All we're going to do is drive by the house. See if it looks occupied. See if Claude's car is in the driveway."

"All right. Okay." Jamie took a few deep, calming breaths. That didn't sound too dangerous. "He won't know this car?"

"This car is brand-new. Just drove it off the lot this morning."

"And it goes from zero to sixty in five seconds, I see. Daniel, seriously, you haven't driven in years. Don't you think this is a bit much for your first outing?"

"It's all coming back to me. Like riding a bicycle. You never forget."

"Fine, but if we get pulled over for speeding—"

"I could outrun a cop."

"Daniel, listen to yourself! What about the new Daniel who insisted on putting quarters in a parking meter because he intended to follow the rules like an ordinary person? Was that all a lie? Do you believe you're above the law? Are you still trying to impress me?"

He was impressing her, all right. His tone, his manner and that determined gleam in his eye impressed her as being just a little bit crazy.

Something she'd said must have gotten through to him, because he did ease off the accelerator. They were still above the speed limit, but not excessively so.

"I just... I've never been this close to finally catching the man who stole six years of my life. My parents' lives. Every waking minute of their last good years was spent trying to prove my innocence. Trying to save my life.

"Claude. Of all people. He was my friend. I brought him into my house, gave him a great job, paid him well, gave him complete freedom to set up the kitchen with the latest equipment, buy the most exotic ingredients, cook anything he could dream up. It's all he ever wanted. Why would he do this?"

Jamie, who had seen all kinds of people commit all kinds of crimes for all kinds of bizarre reasons, had an idea.

"Jealousy. He started a restaurant with you. It failed. Then you went on to own a successful restaurant with Andreas. What better revenge than to kill one partner and frame the other?

"Then, he and Christopher Gables owned a restaurant. It went bankrupt, I'm guessing. Christopher then partnered with Sissom. Their restaurant was a success. It was like slapping Claude in the face with the proof of his inadequacy."

"If he hated me, why did he come to work with me?"

"Maybe as a chance to redeem himself, to show the world that he really was the best chef around? Maybe he was happy. Maybe he didn't hate you, and never would have tried to hurt you…if we hadn't started digging around."

"Exit right," the computerized GPS voice instructed.

Jamie's stomach swooped. They really were going to drive past a house where a murderer resided. A man who wanted Daniel dead, and had very nearly killed her.

"If you're right—if Claude's our man—the metal shavings make sense. He made a big production out of sharpening his knife when he made us Caesar salad."

"He's obsessive about sharpening his knives. Can't believe I didn't see the connection earlier. Listen, there's no reason for you to go anywhere near Claude. I'll drop you off at that Starbucks up ahead."

"No way. I'm not letting you go there alone." She might be the only voice of reason in this car. She had to stop him if he got any crazy notions about confronting his enemy.

Claude's house was just outside the tony Bellaire neighborhood. Lots of trees, upscale shopping and restaurants. As Daniel prepared to turn left onto Templeton Avenue, they had to wait for a tow truck coming the other way, turning right. On the bed of the truck was a blue Renault sedan, crunched in on one side.

As the truck turned, Daniel's jaw dropped. "That's Claude's car. It looks like he really was in a wreck. I thought that was just a cover story to explain why he hadn't come in to work."

"He was in a wreck?"

"His mother called this morning and talked to Jillian. Said he was in a bad accident. Broke his leg, lost an eye—"

"Good Lord."

"I'd already begun to suspect him, and when he couldn't be located, I thought the accident was just a cover story."

They followed the truck at a discreet distance. Templeton Avenue was a street of cute little bungalows that had transformed themselves to upscale. Mature trees, neatly manicured lawns, expensive SUVs and sports cars parked in the driveways all indicated this was a neighborhood that had gone up in value.

The truck stopped in front of a little white cottage with a picket fence and pansies planted around the bright red front door.

Daniel drove by slowly.

"Destination on the right," the GPS lady told them.

He switched it off. "That's the place." He pulled past the house, turned around and parked near the curb a couple of houses down.

"We've seen the house," Jamie said as the tow truck maneuvered into the driveway. "Can we go now?"

"In a minute." Daniel looked alert, like a hunting dog who'd just gotten a whiff of deer.

As the truck's driver got out and began unhitching the Renault, the front door opened and a tiny, white-haired woman tottered outside, leaning heavily on a cane.

"Oh, my God," Daniel said. "Is that Marie? What I wouldn't give for a good pair of binoculars."

"She looks kind of old to be Claude's mother."

"She was near forty when he was born. Anyway, I think she's been sick. If I could see her up close, I would know for sure."

"You've met her?"

"A few times, years ago, when Claude and I had the restaurant. Lots of our recipes were hers. She came into the restaurant on a regular basis to keep an eye on things, make sure her boy was doing everything right."

"Seriously?"

"She was a sweet lady. Harmless. I'm going to talk to her," Daniel said. "I need to figure out what's going on."

"Daniel. Let the police handle this."

"You know, Jamie, the police did not do such a bang-up job investigating Andreas's murder before. You might trust them to take care of things as they should, but sometimes a man has to take matters into his own hands."

Jamie didn't like this. Not at all. "I'm going with you." If Claude had been seriously injured in a car accident, he wouldn't be here, she reasoned. He would be in the hospital. And the frail little old lady didn't look capable of hurting anybody.

Daniel reached into the backseat and grabbed the vase of roses he'd sent to her in the hospital. "Tucker, you stay in the car." He fixed Jamie with his laserlike stare. "You, too. I'll only be a minute." He turned the Jaguar's ignition long enough to crack a window for Tucker. Then he opened his door and climbed out.

"That's bullshit." She quickly exited and walked around the front of the car to join him, whether he wanted her there or not. "You're giving Claude *my* flowers?"

"I'll buy you more."

"You can't solve everything with money. And you can't order me around like one of your house staff."

"I apologize. I'm a little keyed up."

"Ya think? Okay, is it safe or not? If it is, I'm going

with you. If not, we should wait in the car for the police to arrive. Which is it?"

"Just get back in the car. Please," he added.

She didn't, of course. She waited until he'd walked several purposeful steps toward the old woman, who was talking to the truck driver. Then she followed him.

He stopped, turned and stared daggers at her. She stared right back. If not for the situation they were in it would have been comical. Daniel simply wasn't used to people not following his orders.

"Fine," he ground out. "Follow my lead." He took her hand, and they walked together up to the yard.

The woman finally saw them when they were almost upon her. "Mrs. Morel?" Daniel said.

"Yes?" she asked guardedly. Then the light of recognition came into her eyes. "Oh, *mon Dieu,* is it really you, Daniel? It has been so many years." Her voice carried a heavy French accent.

"It's me."

"And you brought such beautiful flowers. But you never... Not since... Claude said you do not leave the estate."

"I heard Claude was injured. He's been a friend for so many years, I had to come see him. I want to be sure he has the care he needs to get better. He's staying here with you, isn't he?"

"He needs someone to take care of him." Mrs. Morel turned her eyes, which were sharp and shrewd despite how frail the rest of her looked, toward Jamie. "And who might this pretty *mademoiselle* be?"

Daniel still held on to Jamie's hand. He raised it and kissed the knuckles. "This is my girlfriend, Jamie."

"I didn't know you had a girlfriend. Not that Claude tells me everything…"

"It's a recent development. Can we see Claude?"

"He is…" Mrs. Morel shook her head sadly. "Not in a good condition for visitors."

Jamie let out a pent-up breath. He was here. But was he truly injured? Or would Claude and his mother bolt for the airport the moment she and Daniel left?

"It's a terrible shame this happened right before your trip to France," Daniel said.

Mrs. Morel blinked in surprise, but quickly schooled her features. "Yes, we were so looking forward to seeing our family. My parents—Claude's grandparents—might not have many years left. And Claude was looking forward to seeing many cousins. We have postponed the trip, of course."

Oh, she was good. Unless…the trip really had been planned in advance, and she didn't realize that Claude had never told Daniel about it. Maybe she had no idea what her son had done. It did seem that the accident, at least, was real.

"Please, Mrs. Morel, I need to see Claude," Daniel said. "I want to personally reassure him that I'll provide the best medical care, rehabilitation, whatever it takes.

And that he will always have a position in my household, whenever he's ready to come back."

"That's very kind of you, but…" Finally she relented. "I'll check. He takes many pain pills. He might be asleep, and I wouldn't want to disturb him."

Mrs. Morel quickly concluded her business with the truck driver, then led the way toward her front door, pausing to stoop down and pinch a dead pansy blossom from a large pot on the front porch.

Jamie squeezed Daniel's hand hard. This wasn't part of the plan.

He leaned down and whispered in her ear. "I just want to see if he's really injured. Ten to one she won't let us see him."

She had a bad feeling about this. Recalling how Daniel's temper had suddenly flared when he'd seen her at the party, she mentally winced. How much worse would it be when he faced the man who'd murdered his friend and set him up to take the rap?

DANIEL'S HEART POUNDED as he crossed the threshold. The man he had hated for so many years, the man he'd vowed to punish, one way or another, was here. So close.

What Daniel chose to do in the next few minutes would dictate Claude Morel's future, as well as his own. Was he up to making that decision?

Certainly Jamie's presence put a kink in the fantasy he'd nurtured, the one-on-one showdown he'd lived over and over in his dreams. Then there was Marie. He couldn't very well assault a critically injured man in front of his mother.

But he was going to do something besides meekly slink away and wait for the police and the lawyers to muck everything up. He would have his day with the man who had stolen his youth, stolen his parents' golden years and sentenced him to six years of hell on earth.

Mrs. Morel's house smelled faintly of garlic and onions, the remnant of the lunch she'd prepared, perhaps. Otherwise, it was neat as a convent, with dainty, elegant furnishings, pastel-pink carpets, bookcases displaying glass figurines. Needlepoint pillows and embroidery samplers were everywhere.

In the living room, where she asked them to wait, was an ancient armchair and a large needlework basket next to it, a half-finished crochet project sitting on top. The TV was on, tuned to a daytime talk show, the volume turned down.

When Mrs. Morel left the room, Jamie nearly came unglued. "Daniel, we shouldn't be here," she whispered. "From a prosecutor's standpoint, I'm telling you this is bad. We could ruin the case against him if we talk to him before the police interrogate him."

"So long as he doesn't know we suspect him, we'll be safe," Daniel reasoned, still not sure where this was going. But he didn't want Jamie making the decisions. This was his fight. "We're here to visit a sick friend, nothing more."

A few minutes passed. Daniel paced, looking out the window. Now that the adrenaline of discovery was wearing off, he began to feel the first faint stirrings of unease. "Maybe you're right. Maybe this wasn't such a good idea."

"Let's leave, then," Jamie said. "Just shout down the hallway that we have to go and we'll get the hell out of here."

Just then, Mrs. Morel reappeared, bearing a tray of cheeses, crackers and sliced apples. "I was just fixing a snack for Claude. Even with all of the fancy dishes he cooks, he still enjoys simple foods—*les frommages, les fruits.*" She set the tray down on the coffee table.

"How is Claude?" Jamie asked, wondering if he was here at all, or if the woman was stalling them for a reason.

"You can ask me. I'm right here." A wheelchair stood poised at the entrance to the living room. Seated in it was Claude—once Daniel's friend, now his enemy—in a checkered flannel bathrobe. His leg extended along the footrest, encased in a metal brace. A huge wad of gauze was taped over his right eye, and his face was bruised and peppered with small cuts.

"Claude. Here, let me help you." His mother rushed to get behind his chair and maneuver it into place in the center of the room.

"Daniel? I couldn't believe it when Mama said you were here." Claude's speech was slurred, probably from pain medication.

Daniel wasn't prepared for the intensity of the emotion welling up inside him. His jaw clenched, and his hands balled themselves into fists. His vision seemed to blur, and for a few seconds he viewed Claude's broken body through a reddish haze. Then his vision cleared and he saw everything with crystal clarity. The clock on the fireplace mantel ticked loud enough to cause an earthquake. His own breathing roared in his ears.

"I'll leave you young people alone to talk," Mrs. Morel said.

"No, please, stay," Jamie said, sounding slightly desperate. "We'll only be a minute. How are you feeling, Claude? It must have been a terrible accident. Look, we brought you some flowers." She picked up the vase from where Daniel had set it down and more or less shoved it at him.

"That's nice. Red roses, Daniel? I didn't know you cared quite that much."

"I'll read the card," Mrs. Morel said, plucking the small florist's envelope from the depths of the bouquet, where it had been hiding.

"No!" Daniel and Jamie said together, realizing their mistake. But the elderly woman was faster than she looked, and she danced away from them as she pulled the card from the envelope.

"Dearest Jamie…"

"I was in a hurry," Daniel said unconvincingly.

"We should go, Daniel," Jamie said. "Claude obviously needs his rest."

"I don't think so." It was Mrs. Morel who spoke. She no longer had the envelope in her hand. She had a handgun almost bigger than she was, and it was pointed straight at Daniel's heart.

CHAPTER FIFTEEN

THE FIRST THING DANIEL DID was shove Jamie behind him. But then he went very still as he considered his options. Claude's mother was a frail old woman, but she was probably strong enough to pull that trigger, and that gun had enough firepower to kill both himself and Jamie with one bullet.

God, what had he gotten them into?

"Mama!" Claude sat up straight in his wheelchair, suddenly much more alert than he'd been before. "What are you doing? I'll handle this."

"But he knows, Claude. Whatever it is you've done that's caused the trouble, he knows about it. I see it in his eyes. He has such a look of hatred." She took a menacing step forward. "You two leave. Now."

"Sure, no problem," Jamie said, taking Daniel's arm and trying to drag him toward the door.

But he was rooted to the floor. "Why, Claude? Just tell me why you would kill a man and let me take the fall."

"I didn't just *let* you take the fall. I made sure you did." Claude worked furiously at the brace on his leg, unfastening buckles and loosening straps. "You were at my apartment, remember? I asked you to carve the roast. Then when no one was looking, I carefully placed the knife in a plastic bag."

"My God, that was months before the murder."

"I planned it for a long time. When I heard you were going into business with Andreas Musto, that untalented fry cook, I couldn't believe it. We could have made it, you and I, Le Bistro. If you'd just been more patient and given my ideas time to come to fruition—"

"You were bleeding us dry, Claude. You seemed to think I had an endless supply of cash, and I didn't."

"Of course you did! Your father was a billionaire."

"My father, not me. He loaned us the money to open the restaurant. I had to pay him back. We had to close the doors because we'd run out of operating capital."

"No. You plotted behind my back with Andreas."

"So why didn't you just kill me?" Daniel asked.

"Because the police would have figured it out. I had a motive. But if I killed Andreas and framed you...it was perfect. I didn't even know the bastard."

"But you left DNA at the scene," Jamie said. "At both scenes. Because you killed Frank Sissom, too."

"You two must be crazy," Mrs. Morel said. "My Claude could never kill anyone."

"Then why were you helping him leave the country?" Daniel demanded.

"He said he'd gotten into some trouble. The car accident—he said he'd crashed with the car of a powerful, angry man. So I make up a little story, that he'd been hurt much worse than he was to buy him a little time so he could get away for a while. He would never hurt anyone on purpose."

The woman sounded on the verge of tears, but the gun never wavered. It was still pointed directly at Daniel.

Claude finally worked the brace free of his leg, which apparently was not injured at all. In one swift move he hoisted himself up and out of the wheelchair, swung the brace over his head, and crashed it into Daniel's head.

The unexpected salvo was enough to stun Daniel, driving him down to one knee.

"Claude, what are you doing?" his mother objected.

"I know what I'm doing, Mama." He ripped the gauze off his perfectly good eye, then grabbed the sharp cheese knife from the tray and hauled Jamie up by her hair. Before Daniel could react, Claude had the knife at Jamie's throat.

"Don't even think of trying anything clever," Claude said. "This knife might be small, but Mama keeps her knives very sharp, just like I do.

"Here's how this is going to work. Daniel, you're going to lie down on the floor. Mama, you're going to tie him up."

"With what?" Mrs. Morel sounded completely lost.

"Use the belt to my robe," Claude said curtly.

Daniel's wits were returning. He had a cut on his cheekbone where the sharp metal from the leg brace had made contact. Blood dripped onto his shirt, and his head throbbed, but otherwise he was okay.

He glanced up. Seeing Jamie's terrified eyes and Claude holding that knife at her throat was almost too much to bear. He wanted to launch himself at Claude and rip his heart out with his bare hands.

But one false move could cost Jamie her life. And God knew whether Mrs. Morel would shoot. A mother's love for her son sometimes transcended sanity.

"What do I do with the gun?" Mrs. Morel said.

"Put it down," Claude answered impatiently. "I've got them covered. The interfering D.A. can't move without getting a sliced jugular. And Daniel—he won't risk her life by disobeying orders. Isn't that right, Daniel?"

"Right," Daniel managed, still crouched, holding his head in his hands, feigning an injury far greater than the reality. Why not use a chapter from Claude's book against him?

Mrs. Morel laid the gun down on the mantel and, moving hesitantly, went to her son and untied the belt of his robe. Daniel knew if he was going to do something, it had to be fast. Once he was tied up, it would be a simple matter for Claude to neutralize Jamie.

But he soon discovered he'd underestimated the woman he loved.

"What are you going to do with us?" Jamie asked.

"I won't kill you unless I have to," Claude said. "Not in my mother's home. Clearly you haven't gone to the police, or they'd be here. If I can slow you down long enough, I'll be away safely."

"To Paris," Jamie said. "We know about the reservations."

While she talked, Daniel moved subtly until he had one shoulder under the coffee table.

"Well, go on, Mama," Claude said. "Tie him up."

Mrs. Morel came up behind him, leaned over and grabbed one of Daniel's wrists. Her grip was surprisingly strong.

Jamie picked that moment to make her move. She grabbed Claude's knife hand and pulled it away from her neck. She was only able to get a couple of inches clearance, but that enabled her to circle-step one foot behind his and unbalance him. As he stumbled, the tip of his knife sliced through Jamie's sweater and into her arm. She screamed as a splash of crimson stained her clothing.

With a roar of fury Daniel rose, bringing the whole coffee table with him, cheese plate, glass figurines and all. He threw all of his weight behind it, smashing it down on Claude, finishing the job Jamie had started.

Daniel lurched to his feet and tossed the upturned table aside with the strength of outrage fueling him. Jamie lunged toward the fireplace, perhaps trying to get her hands on the gun, but Mrs. Morel extended her cane and hooked Jamie's ankle with it.

With a cry of frustration Jamie fell to her knees.

Daniel was on top of Claude now, one hand clamped

over Claude's wrist and beating it against the pink carpet, trying to get him to drop the knife. But the rug beneath them was soft, and Claude stubbornly refused to let go.

Daniel placed a knee in Claude's gut, grabbed half of a broken glass dog, and banged the sharp edge into Claude's knife hand.

Finally the chef released the knife. "All right, all right! For God's sake, man, you've won!"

"I've got the gun, Daniel!" Jamie shouted. "It's over."

But it wasn't, not for Daniel. His fantasy was coming true. He tossed the knife well away, then fitted his hands around Claude's neck. "This is for the six years of hell you put me through." He squeezed. "This is for ruining the last years my parents had on earth." Claude choked as Daniel squeezed harder. "For killing my friend, and for Christopher Gables and Frank Sissom and everyone else whose lives you ruined."

"Daniel, stop! I've got the gun."

He didn't want to stop. He wanted to choke the life out of the bastard.

"Daniel!" she said again, pleading this time. Someone pounded on the door. Mrs. Morel sobbed, pleading for the life of her son.

Daniel looked over his shoulder at Jamie. She had blood all over her. What was he doing? Letting the woman he loved bleed to death so he could get his revenge? How many lives had *he* been about to destroy, just so he could settle a score?

He loosened his hands. Claude gasped for breath.

"Police. We need to talk to you!" It was Abe Comstock on the front porch, bellowing through the door.

Daniel raised himself on one knee. "Jamie, how bad are you hurt?"

"It's not that bad."

"You know how to handle a firearm?"

"Yes. Go get the door."

That turned out to be unnecessary. The front door flew open and a crowd of blue uniforms pushed inside, guns drawn.

Comstock pushed his way to the front and looked around the living room. "Holy mother of— What the hell is going on in here? Jamie, put the gun down!"

She slowly lowered it. "Mrs. Morel pulled a gun on us," Jamie said, sounding ridiculously calm. "Then Claude assaulted Daniel with his leg brace and put a knife to my throat, and Daniel fought back, and I got the gun and here we are."

"If you'd waited ten minutes," Comstock said, "you could have saved yourself a lot of trouble. I had a warrant to arrest Claude Morel. This him?" He pointed to the bleeding man on the floor.

"That's him."

"Somebody call for paramedics." Comstock knelt down, helped Claude to sit up, then promptly snapped handcuffs on him.

Daniel went to Jamie and led her to a chair, urging her into it. "You're not okay. You're bleeding all over the place." The blood had soaked through her sweater halfway down her arm and in a half circle over her torso. He pulled apart the sweater where the knife had cut it, then ripped the sleeve apart.

"Daniel!"

"Honey, you're gushing blood like a geyser." He grabbed one of Mrs. Morel's needlepoint pillows and pressed it against the cut. "Lean back." He'd never seen so much blood. If he didn't stop it, she might bleed out before the paramedics even arrived.

"Thank you, Daniel." She stroked his hair with her free hand.

"Don't thank me yet. This is dicey first aid."

"No, I mean, thank you for not killing Claude. I know you wanted to."

"Part of me wanted to," he admitted. "When I saw that he'd hurt you, everything came rushing back all at once—the pain he'd inflicted on me and my family. I wanted him to feel that pain. But that was the old Daniel, the one who was angry and bitter and wanted an eye for an eye. But the part of me that wants to live—that part was stronger."

"Thank you," she said again.

"You saved me. I heard your voice calling my name, and it brought me back from the brink. I knew if I killed Claude, my life was over, too. If I killed him—even if it was ruled self-defense—I would have lost you. And that was something I couldn't give up, my chance with you, a future with you by my side."

Daniel heard the sirens approaching and knew he had limited time to say what he wanted to say. Once the paramedics came they would take Jamie away, and then the police would have their day, dissecting today's events second by second, trying to decide who was guilty of what.

For all he knew, they might throw him in jail for attempted murder.

That thought didn't upset him as much as it would have only yesterday. If he could just get one thing settled.

"Jamie, beautiful Jamie, you've given me back my life, made me strong again. No matter what happens now, I'll be okay. But do you think we could have a future? Is there hope for us?"

He waited breathlessly for her answer. But when it didn't come, he chanced a look at her.

She had passed out.

FOR THE SECOND TIME in only a few days, Jamie woke up in a hospital emergency room stuck with enough needles to turn her into a pincushion. This time it wasn't Robyn's face she saw when she opened her eyes, though. It was Daniel's.

"Jamie. Dear God."

Her arm throbbed, and she wished for a few seconds she could just sink back into that lovely, hazy nothingness. But Daniel was here; he wasn't a dream. That was his hand holding hers, warm and secure.

"I told you we should have waited in the car," she said.

He smiled through a pained expression. "I will listen to you from now on. I promise. How do you feel?"

"Ready for a dance marathon, can't you tell?" Then she thought to ask, "Am I okay?"

"Nothing a couple of gallons of blood and a whole lot of bed rest won't cure." It wasn't Daniel talking, but Dr. Novak. "I wasn't expecting to see you back here so fast."

"It's not like I was eager to return," Jamie shot back. "And no, I didn't try to cut my wrist and miss."

"You're never going to let me live that down, are you?" Dr. Novak checked the readings on various beeping machines. "Ah, your numbers look a whole lot better than when you came in here."

"Good. Can I go home?"

"Not yet, but it won't be long," Dr. Novak said. "Now, if you'll excuse me, I have rounds to make."

Once they were alone, Daniel took Jamie's hand. "I'm breaking you out of here just as soon as I can," he said. "You're coming home with me. I've appointed myself your twenty-four-hour nurse."

"Mmm, Jillian will love that."

"Jillian has already packed her things and moved out," Daniel admitted. "She said I would be sorry, that without her my life would fall apart. She might be right," he said. "I haven't done a bang-up job running things so far. But I'm sure I'll get better at it. So you'll let me take care of you until you're stronger?"

"Anything to get me out of this place." But once she'd regained her strength, then what? She sighed. "Guess I'll have to get my résumé in order. Who will want to hire a prosecutor who mistakenly put a man on death row?"

"Are you kidding? When the true story comes out, you can write your own ticket. At the very least, Chubb will beg you to come back. But I was kind of hoping you'd come work for me."

"For you, personally?" She hoped he wasn't suggesting she should replace Jillian.

"For Project Justice. As an investigator. You're damn good at it. And we could use another attorney—I rely too much on Raleigh. Whatever the D.A.'s office is paying you, I'll double it."

His offer was tempting—for all of five seconds. She wanted a lot of things, but being Daniel's employee wasn't one of them.

"Daniel, it's not that I don't appreciate the offer or your confidence in me, but I'm a prosecutor. I put bad guys away. It's what I love."

"But we're a team. You have to admit we work well together."

She nodded. "But Project Justice is your dream. And while I admire your passion, it's not mine."

"You're making this hard on me."

"Because I won't fall in line with your plans?"

"You don't remember what we talked about just before you passed out, do you?"

"Um, no. I remember you putting a pillow on my arm."

"Then I'll start over. I want you in my life. Any way I can get you. Offering you a job seemed the most expedient, but not the most effective, I guess."

Jamie's mouth opened, but nothing came out.

"I won't blame you if you walk away. I've been manipulative and high-handed, you've almost died because of me not once, not twice, but three times, and I cost you your job."

"You do show a lady a good time." Jamie's eyes were suddenly awash with tears.

"Oh, dear God, I've made you cry on top of everything else."

"Do you mean it, Daniel? I'm not just a…a diversion, or a novelty you'll get tired of after a while?"

"I wasn't going to bring this up, because I thought it was too much, too soon, but I am so sure that I will never grow tired of you that I want us to get married."

"Oh, boy…" Her tears spilled over. "Now I really am going to cry. I don't cry, Daniel. Nothing ever makes me cry."

He kissed her tears away.

"So are you crying because the answer is 'yes, I want to spend the rest of my life with you'? Or 'no, you're crazy as a bedbug and first chance I get, I'm filing a restraining order'?"

"Daniel. You *are* crazy as a bedbug." She kissed him with a lot more passion than she should have, given her health at the moment, and stopped only when she got light-headed from lack of oxygen. "But I do want to spend the rest of my life with you. I love you, Daniel."

"I love you, Jamie."

They would have kissed again, but the door opened and Abe Comstock entered, looking cocky. "Are you about done in here? I told you five minutes, and it's been fifteen."

"She just woke up," Daniel said with a shrug. Then to Jamie he explained, "I owe him an interview."

"Glad to see you're feeling better, Jamie," Abe said. "Don't get too comfortable. Your turn is next. I sure hope y'all's stories match, 'cause I'm ready for this stinkin' case to be over."

Daniel stood and squeezed her hand. "I'll see you later. Do what the doctor says."

"Yes, Nurse Daniel."

THE PODIUM HAD BEEN SET UP on the front steps of the Harris County courthouse, and Jamie's stomach was filled with butterflies.

It was January, the new year, more than a month since she'd almost died at Claude Morel's hands.

The actions she and Daniel had taken to free Christopher Gables had opened a pretty big can of worms. It had taken a lot of explaining, a lot of interviews. Evidence was checked and cross-checked, stories compared.

In the end, the Houston police and the Harris County district attorney's office had both grudgingly agreed they had made a mistake in sending Christopher Gables to prison. Claude Morel had been charged with two counts of first-degree murder, one count of attempted murder and two counts of felony assault.

Christopher Gables had been released from prison. Although Jamie hadn't talked to him, he had sent her a polite note, through his new attorney, thanking her for her role in his exoneration.

Project Justice had received another round of praise from the media and from various government officials, from the Houston mayor to the president of the United States, and donations for the important work Project Justice did rolled in. Daniel had started coming into work at the office three days a week.

It had taken Jillian exactly forty-eight hours to realize Daniel wasn't going to come crawling back, begging for her to resume her position as his assistant and/or his girlfriend, lover or wife. A penitent, subdued Jillian had asked Daniel for a second chance, doing whatever job he thought she would be good at. He'd offered her a couple of administrative positions at both Project Justice and Logan Oil. In the end she had surprised everyone by asking if she could be an intern at Project Justice, learning to investigate from the ground up.

Daniel had agreed to give it a try.

Jillian had also personally apologized to Jamie for her attitude. She admitted she was wrong about Jamie, and hoped they could someday be friends. Jamie, too happy with Daniel to bear a grudge, had told her all was forgiven.

Everyone in Daniel's circle, both his household staff and his employees, had seemed thrilled by the news of Daniel's engagement. The women, especially, had circled around Jamie, asking if she wanted help planning the wedding and in general trying to make her feel as welcome as possible. They all made it a point to say that her former—and possibly future—occupation didn't bother them.

Now here they all were, gathered around her and Daniel to show their support.

Daniel checked his watch. "It's about that time. Are you nervous?"

"Terrified."

"Me, too."

Daniel still didn't like crowds or closed-in spaces, and she couldn't get him inside a shopping mall. But he'd made remarkable progress since deciding to take back control of his life.

"What if they throw rotten tomatoes?" she asked.

"We'll duck."

At the appointed time, Daniel stepped up to the microphone. "Good morning, and thank you all for coming. I'm Daniel Logan, and this is former Assistant District

Attorney Jamie McNair. We called you here to address a number of issues.

"A lot of rumors have been flying around since the arrest of Claude Morel. You've had to rely on often conflicting and confusing police reports as well as a lot of 'unnamed sources close to the story' who frankly didn't know what they were talking about.

"So here's the skinny. Ms. McNair and I cooperated in the investigation that led to Morel's arrest and the overturn of Christopher Gables's conviction. Jamie was dismissed from the district attorney's staff as a result of philosophical differences over this case.

"Yes, Jamie and I both sustained minor injuries when we… When I made the unwise decision to confront a man who was cornered and desperate. But as you can plainly see, neither of us is in a coma on life support, neither of us has brain damage and Jamie still has both of her arms."

The crowd laughed a bit. Daniel was making reference to a couple of tabloid stories showing badly doctored photos of Jamie with only one arm, and Daniel in a hospital bed, hooked up to machines.

"How did you figure out Claude was the murderer?" one of the reporters shouted out.

"We can't comment on that—it's an ongoing investigation. In fact, we've told you pretty much all we can on that subject. So let's move on. Jamie has something she'd like to say."

Jamie stepped up to the podium.

"Good morning. The events of the last few weeks have brought home to me a few truths about crime and punishment—namely, things may not always be what they appear, and sometimes there are no right answers. As an assistant district attorney I wielded a lot of power. I had the ability to save lives by putting murderers behind bars and to ruin lives if I put the wrong person in prison.

"No one is immune to mistakes. Not cops, not judges and certainly not district attorneys. As you know, Harris County District Attorney Winston Chubb has announced he will leave office in May, before his term is up. There will be a special election held to fill the vacancy. This morning, I am announcing my candidacy. If elected, what I will bring to the office is an open mind. A commitment to looking for the right answers, even when they're not easy. A willingness to admit mistakes when they're made, and correct them.

"I'll have more specifics about my platform in the coming days and weeks. But right now, I'd like to change the subject one more time. Daniel?"

Daniel took the microphone again. "Rumors have been swirling for weeks now about the supposed relationship between myself and Jamie McNair. I want to be very clear about this. The rumors are absolutely... true. We are, in fact, engaged to be married."

Jamie was ready to step down. They had agreed that they wouldn't give out any details about their approaching nuptials.

But Daniel kept talking.

"I'm sure some of you think it's odd, that we're on different sides of the fence and how could that work? We'll keep each other on our toes, that's for sure. But I just want you to know, Jamie is the most wonderful thing to come into my life. She is passionate about her work, but she is filled with compassion, as well. I believe those qualities will serve her well—as district attorney, and as my wife.

"To you naysayers, I will add that I love this woman more than life itself. Love can overcome an awful lot. I'm living proof."

He hugged her and she hugged him back, heedless of how mushy they looked.

"Damn it, Daniel," she whispered in his ear, "you're making my mascara run in front of the TV cameras."

"You'll thank me later," he whispered back. "Listen to that applause. I just got you elected."

Maybe she'd win the election, maybe she wouldn't. It didn't matter. With Daniel at her side, she was already a winner.

* * * * *

COMING NEXT MONTH

Available May 10, 2011

#1704 A FATHER'S QUEST
Spotlight on Sentinel Pass
Debra Salonen

#1705 A TASTE OF TEXAS
Hometown U.S.A.
Liz Talley

#1706 SECRETS IN A SMALL TOWN
Mama Jo's Boys
Kimberly Van Meter

#1707 THE PRODIGAL SON
Going Back
Beth Andrews

#1708 AS GOOD AS HIS WORD
More Than Friends
Susan Gable

#1709 MITZI'S MARINE
In Uniform
Rogenna Brewer

You can find more information on upcoming
Harlequin® titles, free excerpts and more at
www.HarlequinInsideRomance.com.

HSRCNM0411

*With an evil force hell-bent on destruction,
two enemies must unite to find a truth that turns
all-too-personal when passions collide.*

*Enjoy a sneak peek in Jenna Kernan's next installment
in her original* TRACKER *series, GHOST STALKER,
available in May, only from Harlequin Nocturne.*

"**W**ho are you?" he snarled.

Jessie lifted her chin. "Your better."

His smile was cold. "Such arrogance could only con
from a Niyanoka."

She nodded. "Why are you here?"

"I don't know." He glanced about her room. "I asked tl
birds to take me to a healer."

"And they have done so. Is that *all* you asked?"

"No. To lead them away from my friends." His eyes flu
tered and she saw them roll over white.

Jessie straightened, preparing to flee, but he rous
himself and mastered the momentary weakness. His ey
snapped open, locking on her.

Her heart hammered as she inched back.

"Lead who away?" she whispered, suddenly afraid
the answer.

"The ghosts. Nagi sent them to attack me so I wou
bring them to her."

The wolf must be deranged because Nagi did not ser
ghosts to attack living creatures. He captured the evil on
after their death if they refused to walk the Way of Soul
forcing them to face judgment.

"Her? The healer you seek is also female?"

"Michaela. She's Niyanoka, like you. The last Seer
Souls and Nagi wants her dead."

Jessie fell back to her seat on the carpet as the possibility this ricocheted in her brain. Could it be true?

"Why should I believe you?" But she knew why. His ack aura, the part that said he had been touched by death. aly a ghost could do that. But it made no sense.

Why would Nagi hunt one of her people and why would Skinwalker want to protect her? She had been trained from rth to hate the Skinwalkers, to consider them a threat.

His intent blue eyes pinned her. Jessie felt her mouth go y as she considered the impossible. Could the trickster be eaking the truth? Great Mystery, what evil was this?

She stared in astonishment. There was only one way to d her answers. But she had never even met a Skinwalker fore and so did not even know if they dreamed.

But if he dreamed, she would have her chance to learn e truth.

Look for GHOST STALKER by Jenna Kernan, available May only from Harlequin Nocturne, wherever books and ebooks are sold.

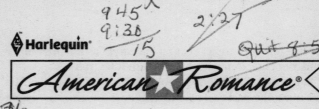

Harlequin
American ★ Romance

Fan favorite author
TINA LEONARD
is back with
an exciting new miniseries.

Six bachelor brothers are given a challenge—
get married, start a big family and whoever does
so first will inherit the famed Rancho Diablo.
Too bad none of these cowboys is marriage material!

> # *Callahan Cowboys:*
> ### Catch one if you can!

The Cowboy's Triplets (May 2011)
The Cowboy's Bonus Baby (July 2011)
The Bull Rider's Twins (Sept 2011)
Bonus Callahan Christmas Novella! (Nov 2011)
His Valentine Triplets (Jan 2012)
Cowboy Sam's Quadruplets (March 2012)
A Callahan Wedding (May 2012)